A Heart in Flight

*Also by Nina Coombs Pykare
in Large Print:*

The Haunting of Grey Cliffs

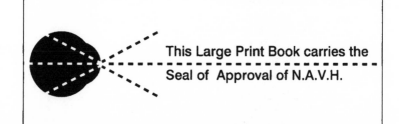

A Heart in Flight

Nina Coombs Pykare

Thorndike Press • **Waterville, Maine**

Published in 2001 by arrangement with
Maureen Moran Agency.

Thorndike Press Large Print Candlelight Series.

The tree indicium is a trademark of Thorndike Press.

The text of this Large Print edition is unabridged.
Other aspects of the book may vary from the original edition.

Set in 16 pt. Plantin by Al Chase.

Printed in the United States on permanent paper.

Library of Congress Cataloging-in-Publication Data
Pykare, Nina.
    A heart in flight / Nina Coombs Pykare.
      p. cm.
    ISBN 0-7862-3466-0 (lg. print : hc : alk. paper)
    1. Hot air balloons — Fiction. 2. Large type books.
  I. Title.
  PS3566.Y48 H43 2001
  813'.54—dc21   2001027762

for William

Chapter

One

April 1819

Spring had come to London, and the streets were abustle with residents greeting the return of warmth to the land. Fashionable bonnets decorated the city's better districts as ladies young and old joyfully went about their various errands.

Aurelia Amesley, entering Hyde Park on the arm of her cousin Harold, surveyed the crowd with sparkling eyes. After the long winter months closeted in their rooms, she felt exhilarated to be part of London's activity once more. And, what was even more exciting, the lasting good weather meant that soon they could have an ascension.

She adjusted her bonnet, a dull affair with a single pink ribbon rosette, which still had years of wear in it, and looked around her.

Hyde Park was crowded. All the swells were out, enjoying the warm weather, expensively clad ladies gracing their arms. Aurelia smiled. Let the swells have their ladies. And the ladies their swells. She had something far better.

"Ain't it a great day?"

"Yes, Harold. Yes, it is. Thank you for bringing me to the park."

"Wait'll you see her," Harold said. "She's a real beauty. The best yet."

Harold's brilliant red hair stood up almost straight in the breeze. Under a multitude of freckles, his face glowed with pleasure. He would never make a hero like those in the romances she read to liven the long winter hours — she was fairly certain such men did not exist. But Harold was a good man to have for a cousin. And he knew his aeronautics.

She, too, was excited about the new balloon, the one they'd dreamed of and planned for all winter long. But Harold would get to go up in it.

"This balloon's a great deal bigger," he was saying. "And made of more durable silk. It should travel . . ."

Ordinarily, Aurelia would have been as engrossed as he. But it had been a long hard winter. She'd been cooped up for days on end.

Consequently she let her eyes stray past Harold's head, idly surveying the people out to enjoy the park. Suddenly she found herself looking into a pair of vivid blue eyes.

Their owner held her gaze for several seconds of lazy amusement before he smiled slightly and turned back to his friends.

Aurelia felt the color flooding her cheeks. That dandy certainly didn't have any manners. But she'd learned long ago to ignore such men. The daughter of a wealthy merchant was fair game to their likes. Thank goodness, she was now four and twenty, past her prime, and the fops and fribbles left her to her own devices.

This man, though, didn't look like a fop. Or a fribble. He looked . . . The thought registered with an extra little beat of her heart. Why, he looked like the hero in a Lady Incognita book.

The shoulders under his blue coat of superfine stretched the material taut with their wideness. Curling over the collar of his coat and contrasting with his white cravat was an abundance of curly black hair. But it wasn't his shoulders or his hair — though both fit the mold admirably — but his face that had quite imprinted itself upon her mind.

Although they had locked glances only momentarily, she retained quite a clear picture in her mind. Brilliant blue eyes set under luxuriant black brows. A bold Roman nose. A chin that fairly cried determination.

A mouth, curled in lazy amusement, full-lipped and somehow exciting.

It was clear from his overall appearance that the man was a real out-and-outer. Everything about him, from his insolent gaze to his gleaming black top boots, spoke of the highest quality. But his face showed the signs of living. He must already have seen the far side of thirty.

Forget the dark stranger. There were many interesting people in the park. Strolling along beside Harold, she turned her consideration to the fashionable ladies around them. Their expensive gowns, of jaconet, spotted cambric and muslin, striped silk or sarcenet, were bright and colorful. Even the pelisses and spencers were light and cheerful. They made a pretty picture. But how foolish to spend good money on the fripperies of fashion. Especially when that same money could be spent on advancing the fascinating science of air flight.

Her own gown of bombazine was quite sufficient. And her bonnet . . . She could not remember how old it was. But it was still good.

Mama had been the one with the passion for the pretty clothes. Sometimes, usually in the spring, Aurelia did think of a new gown or two. And Papa had left more than enough money for that. But when the balloons could go up, who wanted to think about fashion foolishness? Except now, since the gentleman had looked at her — and like that — she rather wished she'd had on something new.

Oh well, it was spring. She was simply feeling the season.

The gentleman and his friends were only a few paces ahead. Unaccountably, she could not forbear staring at the man's broad shoulders. They were so wide, and his coat was extremely well-tailored. So broad were his shoulders, in fact, that they effectively blocked the rest of the group from her sight.

Strange that she should be fascinated with this man. Usually, she thought very little of men. Unless, of course, they knew about air flight. But that thinking was not of the same fashion.

She pushed at a curl that had escaped her bonnet and then decided to leave it be. She did rather pride herself on her hair. The color of gold Papa had called it. And for Papa gold was the ultimate compliment.

"There she is!" Harold turned right abruptly, bringing Aurelia around with something of a start. She'd do better to think about the present. Papa and Mama were both gone. But she was fortunate to have Uncle Arthur and Harold, and doubly fortunate they should share her passion for balloon flight.

And there stood the current love of Harold's life — the new balloon he had brought her to admire. The chest-high wicker basket they called the *gondola* seemed almost too fragile to hold human beings. But Harold insisted it was very strong. And the huge, garishly colored balloon from which it hung suspended was really quite safe.

With a smile, Aurelia thought of Mama. Poor Mama hadn't approved of Papa's interest in air flight. But that hadn't stopped Papa. And it wouldn't stop her. If she could ever get Uncle Arthur to listen to reason.

There was such a wild beauty about the balloon. It tugged gently at its ropes, like some great creature wanting to fly free. Aurelia pulled in a breath. She wanted so much to be up in it. To soar . . .

"I say, Harold. That *is* you!"

The deep rich voice came from behind them. Harold turned, taking Aurelia with him. He did it so quickly that she lost her balance and had to reach out with her other hand.

But it was not Harold's arm upon which her fingers closed, but that of the blue-eyed gentleman. For a moment Aurelia stood almost paralyzed.

"Easy there," the gentleman said, covering her gloved hand with his. Again she found herself gazing into those vivid blue eyes. How strange that she could not seem to tear her gaze away.

Indeed, it was his eyes that moved first, sliding down over the black shawl and her dress, then back up to the bonnet with its pink ribbon rosette, before they settled on her face.

He smiled then, a lazy insolent smile that made her hackles rise instantly. She had seen that smile before. She was not some common street girl, and she would not be treated as such. She withdrew her hand and turned to Harold. But he actually seemed to know the man and, beyond that, to be glad to see him!

"Aurelia Amesley," Harold said. "This here's the Earl."

Aurelia stared. "The Earl?" she repeated numbly. How and where had Harold met an Earl?

The Earl smiled, those blue eyes still so warm. "Philip, Earl of Ranfield." He bowed slightly. "I'm pleased to make your acquaintance, Miss Amesley. Very pleased."

Aurelia nodded. She did have some manners, after all.

Ranfield reached out for her gloved hand and raised it to his lips. And she blushed as fiercely as any green girl. How strange. No man had ever made her blush before.

"So," the Earl said, his voice pleasantly deep. "Harold didn't tell me he knew such a beautiful woman."

Harold grinned. She could not believe with what ease the usually shy Harold addressed this lord.

"Reely's m'cousin," Harold said. "Don't actually *see* relatives. "

Why must Harold use that stupid nickname, and in front of an Earl? But he didn't even seem to notice.

"I know," Ranfield said. "Your heart belongs to that beauty over there." He gestured toward the balloon.

Harold nodded. "Yeah, listen. I want to go talk to the men. Whyn't you keep Reely company?"

"But Harold . . ." Aurelia's protest elicited another sheepish smile from her cousin. But it did little else.

"I won't be long. Honest."

Aurelia swallowed an unladylike exclamation as Harold loped off. How unkind of him to leave her with a strange gentleman. And one who looked at her so . . .

"Your cousin's a likable chap."

This comment, when she was thinking thoughts that would have burned her cousin's ears, so startled her that she raised her gaze to the Earl's. And then she could think of nothing to say but, "Yes, he is."

For a moment there was silence between them. Ranfield let himself consider Harold's cousin. What a wide-eyed little miss she was. Pretty, too, in a quiet way — with that heart-shaped face and those great dark eyes in such contrast to the golden hair. But what sensible dull clothes. No flibberti-gibbet charmer, this.

"Do you share Harold's interest in things aeronautical?" he inquired.

"Oh yes."

"Have you been up?"

"I?" Regretfully she shook her head. "No. But, oh, I should like to. I should like it above all else."

His eyebrow rose. Did she really mean she preferred air flight to new gowns, to balls, to routs? "Above all else?" he repeated.

"Yes. Of course."

Her tone was sober, no hint of flirtation. She might have been speaking to her vicar. Was it possible she didn't *know* him? Surely every young woman in London had heard of the wealthy Earl of Ranfield. Enough of them had been scouting after him.

He summoned the smile reputed to melt even the hardest London lady's heart. And Aurelia Amesley calmly asked, "How did you meet Cousin Harold?"

He swallowed a chuckle. That would teach him to have such an inflated opinion of himself.

"It is quite simple," he explained. "I have an intense interest in things aeronautical."

She could not quite countenance that. "But how? You're an earl."

What a refreshing little thing. So straightforward. "I assure you, even an earl can have legitimate interests. Though I fear that ballooning is at present only a hobbyhorse with me, I am considering giving it much more of my time."

Reaching into his pocket, he drew out his snuffbox. The ladies always admired it. "Yes, I think air flight has great possibilities. I had this made up special. Only one of its kind."

Aurelia took the proffered box. She had never seen one decorated in this fashion. As she reached for it, her gloved fingers brushed against his. The ensuing sensation was both pleasant and alarming. She covered her confusion by bending to examine the delicate cloisonnéed lid, upon which a gaily colored balloon floated against an azure sky. "It's lovely."

Aware now that it was not wise to touch him, she tried to hand the box back without making contact. But the Earl's fingers closed around hers. "Not nearly as lovely as you."

The blood insisted on rising to her cheeks. It was rather like Lady Incognita's latest romance. Where the heroine first met the hero — and her heart began to palpitate. Though, of course, *her* heart did not do any such foolish thing.

It was just that it had been a long time since a man had paid her compliments. And they'd always made her uncomfortable. But she was aware that this time, under the discomfort, she was also feeling pleasure.

She tried to give him the benefit of the doubt. He was probably behaving in his normal fashion. Compliments — false, true, what difference did it make? — fell quite naturally from the lips of the *ton*'s Corinthians. It was probably second nature with him to make any — and every — woman feel special.

But why couldn't the man discuss something sensible — say something about the newest balloons or the newest gas for propelling them? "Have you read about Monsieur Charles's attempts with gas?" she asked, finally succeeding in disengaging her fingers from his.

His smile was rueful. She liked it even better than his other rakish one. "I'm afraid not. I am just newly come to the mysteries of aeronautical flight. But I am eager to learn."

"Then perhaps . . ."

"Ho, Ranfield. What have you here?"

Aurelia turned. Oh no, another gentleman. And just when this one had promised to turn a little interesting.

She saw a *moue* of distaste flit across the Earl's face. "Hello, Alvanley."

"Ain't you going to make me acquainted?"

A muscle twitched in his lordship's jaw. Aurelia noted it with surprise. Something had put his lordship's back up. And that something had to do with this other lord.

"This is Miss Amesley, Harold's cousin."

Alvanley's smile turned wolfish. So that was it. She put on her iciest look, but he didn't seem to notice.

"Hmmm. Might be interested in air flight m'self. Any more where she came from?"

Ranfield turned to her. "Miss Amesley, will you excuse us for a moment?"

She had a notion to tell him that she knew just what to do with Alvanley's kind. She was no stranger to the set down, properly delivered. But then, somehow, there popped into her mind a scene from Lady Incognita's latest book — a scene in which the hero rescued the heroine from some villain's calumny.

"Of course." She lowered her eyes, demurely, as a heroine would. Could that Alvanley possibly think she was going to be Ranfield's newest ladybird?

She had never considered such an affiliation. She had hardly even considered marriage, since she knew no man she could envision living with and loving as one should. But she could see how easily some women might decide to fall, especially with Ranfield there to catch them.

Though she had turned away, she could not help overhearing the men.

"Don't appreciate this kind of thing," the Earl was saying.

Alvanley's laugh made her hands tighten into fists. That man needed a good facer.

"Don't suppose Sweet Annette's gonna 'preciate it either. Or is it the Little Dove again?"

The Earl's voice deepened. "My private affairs are just that — private. And I'll thank you to remember it."

Alvanley laughed again. "Private? All of

London's speculating. Why, you've made the betting book at White's. I put my money on your staying free. Can't imagine the likes of you getting leg-shackled. But now this little mouse . . ."

"Miss Amesley is a thoroughly respectable young woman." The Earl's voice held more than a hint of steel. "If I hear her name bandied about . . . anywhere. You will have cause to regret it."

There was a pause. Aurelia debated stepping even farther away, but something held her in place. She was rather enjoying this, her first experience at playing the heroine. However temporarily she might hold the role, she didn't want to miss any of it.

"Right, right, old chap." Alvanley's voice was plainly conciliatory. "I didn't see a thing. But Ranfield, this here's Hyde Park. I ain't the only man about with eyes."

"Good day, Alvanley."

"G'day to you."

Aurelia kept her eyes focused on the balloon. So, this was how the heroine felt when the hero rode to her rescue. Her heart wanted to beat faster. And she wanted to smile at the hero like some silly green girl.

"Sorry to have left you unescorted for so long," the Earl said, returning to her side. "Alvanley's a bore."

"I would have thought you had much in common." The remark escaped her unaware, and only the Earl's raised eyebrow showed her her mistake. Now she'd gone and insulted the man.

"Touché," he said, smiling pleasantly.

She flushed. "I didn't mean . . ."

"Yes, you did." His smile didn't waver. "You have wit as well as looks. Don't deny it."

There wasn't much she could return to that. It was certainly pleasant to have someone think her intelligent. Uncle Arthur was discouragingly prone to treat her like some half-witted child, especially when she mentioned going up in the balloon.

Again she found herself looking into the Earl's eyes. Their magnetism pulled at her; deep dark pools, inviting, beckoning. Warmth trembled over her, and she fought to control the sudden shaking of her knees. Oh, these hero-types were patently dangerous.

"There you are." Harold's voice broke the spell. Aurelia and the Earl turned together.

"Listen, Reely, the men need me."

"Harold, you . . ."

"I know!" Harold grinned. "Ranny can take you to the Minerva."

For a moment, Aurelia could not find her tongue. She admitted to herself that the prospect of more time in the Earl's company was pleasing. But the man had been imposed upon enough. He would be wanting to get away.

But to her surprise, the Earl said, "I'd be greatly pleased to escort Miss Amesley to the lending library." He actually sounded like he meant it. And he offered her his arm.

"Harold, I can't . . ."

But Harold wasn't listening. "Thanks, Ranny. See you later."

Aurelia stared after him in utter frustration. Harold was such a nincompoop. How could he just walk off and leave her like that? This man had other things to do.

She swallowed hastily and forced herself to turn back to the Earl. "There's no need for you to put yourself out," she said, schooling her voice to calmness. "I shall take a hackney to the Minerva."

The Earl straightened and his jaw tightened. It was really quite a handsome jaw. "You shall do no such thing," he said.

"Really, milord."

"Miss Amesley, I will brook no resistance in this matter. Your cousin left you to my care. I would be remiss to neglect my responsibility."

She was perfectly able to take care of herself. But it was kind of him. "Really, milord. I am not your responsibility. I am scarcely a green . . ."

The Earl took her hand and drew it through his arm. "Miss Amesley, you are wasting your breath. Come, my carriage is waiting outside the gate."

It *would* be nice to have a carriage ride. They seldom bothered with niceties like that. Uncle Arthur said walking was good for the constitution *and* the pocket. And he was quite correct. After all, air flight was not a pursuit to be financed on pin money.

In spite of herself, she glanced down at her clothes. The Earl was quite a pattern card of perfection. Not ostentatious, of course. But just so nicely turned out.

While her gown . . . But her clothes were quite presentable. Just because she didn't look like the ladies around her . . . After all, the Earl of Ranfield was talking to *her*, not to any of those fashionably dressed females.

Ranfield frowned. "I apologize for Alvanley. The man has no tact." He smiled. "But really, being seen with me is not the worst fate in the world."

Indeed, it was not. It was turning into a rare treat. So she let him guide her through the crowds and out to a carriage that was, quite as it should be, the highest state of fashion.

The tiger up behind gave her one slightly bemused look. No doubt he was accustomed to more fashionably turned out ladies. But she gave him a smile anyway. Then the Earl handed her up with all the consideration any woman could desire. In fact, his fingers lingered around hers for so long that her heart started getting those funny notions again.

Chapter

Two

Some time later the carriage stopped before 33 Leadenhall Street. In the niche above the door stood the Statue of Minerva. With her spear in one hand and her shield in the other, the helmeted goddess stood guard over the Press and Lending Library which bore her name.

The Earl smiled as he handed her down, that smile that said so much. And made Aurelia *feel* even more. How strange that he should have such an effect on her. But then, it had been a long winter and she had consumed many, many romances. Probably some of that had colored her perception of him.

"Thank you for the ride." She endeavored to speak calmly, but it was difficult. Who would have thought that just being near a man could be so exciting? "I shall be here some time, and then I have other errands to attend to. So you needn't wait." That was only fair. They had imposed on the man enough.

Ranfield nodded. "I shall just escort you inside."

She wanted him to do that, but she didn't want him to know she wanted it. "I . . ."

"There are several books I wish to borrow for myself."

So Aurelia took the arm he offered her. A pleasantly warm sensation stole over her at the feel of it under her fingertips. Was this the sensation Lady Incognita's heroines described?

She much wanted to leave her hand there, to feel so pleasant for a little longer. But she did have some sense of propriety. Papa had not wasted all the money he spent on Miss Rutherford.

So, immediately after they were inside the door, she removed her hand, saying formally, "Good day, milord. And thank you again."

"Good day, Miss Amesley."

For a brief moment she experienced disappointment that he had not continued their conversation. The feeling was almost as bad as when they had called off that ascension last year.

Perhaps it was even worse. Her insides were all aboil. And, unaccountably, she wanted to sniffle.

She turned away, and, conscious of his

eyes following her, moved off into the shelves of books.

It took some moments, once she was out of his sight, to compose herself. She did not, after all, have many days like this one! Imagine meeting a flesh and blood hero. The more she thought about it, the more she felt certain of his "hero-hood."

Well, it was a pleasant memory, something to think on during the cold winter nights when the men had gone to their beds and she couldn't sleep.

She took several deep calming breaths, and, smoothing her skirts, made her way to the shelf that held Lady Incognita's romances. Of course, she had long ago admitted to herself that her passion for such literary fare might be considered unwise.

In spite of Papa's predilection for flight, he had insisted that she receive a good education. And one of the things that Miss Rutherford had determined that her charge commit to memory was the revered Dr. Samuel Johnson's comments on the novel.

Aurelia recited them to herself: "These books are written chiefly to the young, the ignorant, and the idle, to whom they serve as lectures of conduct, and introduction to life." Well, that seemed true enough. Unlike a romance, a novel was supposed to be real.

"Vice," the good doctor continued, "(for vice is necessary to be shown) should always disgust." That was true, too. "It is therefore to be steadily inculcated that virtue is the highest proof of understanding, and the only solid basis of greatness, and that vice is the natural consequence of narrow thoughts, that it begins in mistake, and ends in ignominy."

As long as Miss Rutherford had remained in residence, no romances, and only the best novels (and consequently the very dullest), had come within Aurelia's ken. Human nature being what it is, her desire for the forbidden had only quickened. So as soon as she found herself without supervision, Aurelia had immersed herself in novels of the wrong sort and in numerous romances of terror.

She was well aware that the problems dramatized in romances seldom presented themselves in normal everyday occurrence. And a life spent in haunted castles and abbeys, amongst ghosts and villains, could hardly be considered felicitous.

Still, she did enjoy romances. She liked that world of villains so evil they make one's blood run cold, of heroines helpless and beautiful, of heroes handsome, strong, and victorious. It was a world much more interesting than her own, especially in the winter when their experiments in air flight were made impossible by inclement weather.

She made her way to the familiar shelf that held Lady Incognita's works. Of all the writers of romances of terror, she preferred those of the unknown and mysterious Lady Incognita. Her eyes slid over the titles till they came to rest for a moment on *Love in the Ruins*, which she had returned on her last visit. The triumph of Reginald and Bernice over the villainous monk Columbo had thrilled her to the core. And, even though she knew the outcome of *The Dark Stranger*, she looked forward to reading it again.

A slight noise made her start and look up. A short distance away, leaning against the wall, stood the Earl of Ranfield. He smiled lazily and gave her a slight bow.

Aurelia turned away. Why was the man still in the library? And more important, why was he watching her? It was common knowledge that rakes would stop at nothing to get what they wanted. But what could he want? Perhaps she was going to find out.

So, said Ranfield to himself, she had seen him. He detached himself from the wall and advanced toward her. "Miss Amesley, we meet again."

She met this comment with silence, but, since she did not give him the cut direct, he continued. "I see that you are looking at Lady Incognita's romances. I confess to reading one now and then."

"You read romances!"

How did she widen those great dark eyes like that? And, more to the point, could she possibly be unaware of their effect upon a man?

"I do," he declared. "Why not?"

"I thought . . . that is, a gentleman . . ." She floundered to a halt.

"A gentleman may enjoy a little escape." What could he say to keep her talking? "Also, the heroes of such pieces may give one an idea of what appeals to the ladies."

She raised an eyebrow, a sweet golden eyebrow.

"I hardly think anyone is going to be called upon to rescue fair maidens from dire villains these days."

"Touché," he replied. She was a quick-witted little thing. "How pleasant it is to see you smile. I feared you were one of those dreadful bluestockings who are always pre-dicting calamity."

Her smile vanished. "There is nothing

wrong with a woman using the brains God has given her."

"Of course not, provided He did give her some." He saw instantly that he was in the suds and hastened to add, "I am only joking, of course. I have nothing against learned ladies."

How could such a little thing look so icy? "I humbly beg your pardon. I meant no disrespect to the ladies. Truly I didn't."

Against her better judgment, Aurelia looked up and found his eyes upon her. Strange, how a man's eyes could impart so much warmth.

"Am I to be forgiven?"

She shrugged. "I do not see what difference my forgiveness makes."

"I want it." The words were low and accompanied by another lazy smile that said much more than words could ever convey. It said so much that she found herself actually yearning toward him.

Miss Rutherford's vivid warnings came immediately to mind. So this was the way the rakes operated. No wonder it was so effective. But this one had overestimated his charm. She might have a palpitating heart, but her brains were still in prime condition.

She made her tone deliberately sharp. "You presume too much, milord."

He nodded ingratiatingly. "A frequent mistake of mine. Will you forgive me?"

She wanted to be angry, she should be angry, but that was to no avail. He was really very good at this sort of thing. And she was sadly out of her depth. "Yes," she said shortly, turning back to the shelf.

The man was intoxicating. He made her feel . . . Yes, that was it. He made her feel as she had imagined she would feel *up there*. Breathless and awestruck. Soaring higher and higher.

This was the outside of enough! No *man* was going to make her feel things like that. She moved away from him.

He followed immediately. "Yes," he said. "I find nothing more relaxing than a nice romp with a knight and his lady as they extricate themselves from the toils of a despicable villain."

"I should think a man of your stature would wish to occupy himself with other, more important, things." The memory of his conversation with Alvanley returned, and she colored.

He didn't seem to notice. "I do sometimes read for the edification of my mind," he replied soberly. "But even in doing that I must be most careful."

"How so?" She could not help being interested. Uncle Arthur and Harold scoffed at her romances. Neither one had ever so much as opened a novel and certainly not a romance.

"If I read novels," he said, "I am endangering my character. Unless, of course, I choose them carefully."

Aurelia had to smile. He *did* know Dr. Johnson. "I hardly think Dr. Johnson had men of your stamp in mind. You are neither young nor ignorant."

"Nor idle," he added with that charming grin.

"Nor are you so impressionable as to take an erroneous view of the world from such works." She banished her smile and tried to keep her expression severe. This was not a matter for laughter, but for serious discussion.

"You are right enough about that," said the Earl, moving slightly closer. "I have been in the town for some time. However, this is the first I have ever encountered a woman conversant with Dr. Johnson's theories on the novel."

"And you are the first man I have known who . . ." Her tongue seemed to get twisted in itself, and she could not finish.

He did not seem to mind. "Ah, we have something, then, in common. Besides our passion for things aeronautical."

When he used the word passion, he smiled at her again. It was only a smile, a lazy sort of expression, but she clasped the book that she held tightly, hoping to still the quivering of her fingers. No wonder the Earl did so well with the ladies; few women lived who could resist such a man.

Of course, he was only playing with her. This was probably his usual attitude with women. But he had mistaken his game.

Although the pleasures of love had so far been denied her, she could not consider indulging in them without benefit of matrimony. And certainly matrimony was a far cry from what the Earl's eyes proposed.

"I should still be happy to give you a ride home," he said pleasantly.

She shook her head. The afternoon had been enjoyable. Too enjoyable, in sober fact. Now it was time to be sensible. And the sensible thing was to cut this short. "No, thank you. As I said, I have several errands to do." It was a lie, of course, but surely one was allowed a small lie in such a situation.

Ranfield found, inexplicably, that he did not want this conversation to end. She was different. She was entertaining. She was . . .

"I should be happy to put the services of

my carriage at your disposal."

Again she shook her head. "No, thank you."

She was stubborn, too. "Miss Amesley. Be sensible."

She turned ice maiden. Evidently he had said the wrong thing. Maybe it was that word — *sensible.*

"Has it ever occurred to you that I might not enjoy your company?"

"No." He kept his smile cheerful, that smile that had served him so well for so long. "Actually, my experience has convinced me that women find my companionship desirable. Indeed, they are even apt to go to some trouble to acquire it."

She bit her lip, but the icy look remained. "You are quite insufferable. And exceedingly high in the instep."

"I know," he agreed, waiting for her smile to break. "But I cannot help it; it's part of my considerable charm."

She didn't smile; she frowned. "Milord, since you refuse to take even a broad hint, I am forced to be quite plain. I do not desire your company. Neither today nor at any other time."

It struck him quite forcibly that perhaps she was not playing a game, not trading *bon mots* like ladies of the *ton*. Perhaps she had taken a distinct dislike to him.

The thought was decidedly unpleasant. He refused to consider it further. No woman had ever persisted in refusing him. Still, he must act the gentleman. If she said she didn't want to see him, he must believe her. For the moment.

He bowed from the waist, formally. "I beg your pardon. I shall not bother you any further." And then he marched away, his back straight beneath the well-tailored coat.

For some moments Aurelia stood, staring at the titles through a blur of sudden tears. She had really offended him, and she could not help being sorry. Their conversation had been the most enjoyable she'd had in a long time. It was too bad to have driven him away.

Miss Rutherford would have been proud of her, though, giving him a set down like that. A little smile came to Aurelia's lips. Miss Rutherford would have had some choice phrases about behaving like a green schoolroom girl. The Earl had probably been plagued with *ennui* and had used their chance meeting as a little diversion. Something to wile away an afternoon. By tomorrow he would have forgotten all about it. And so would she.

So she gathered up *The Dark Stranger*, selected another volume by a Miss Eliza Museat, entitled *Cave of Corenza*, and made her way to the desk. She did not look around her, and, even if she had, the tall man watching her from the shadows of a remote corner would probably not have caught her eye. So, when she stepped through the door and out into the spring air, she had no idea that the Earl of Ranfield was smiling thoughtfully, and looking not at all like a man who had just received a proper set down.

By the time Aurelia reached the second floor rooms off Bloomsbury Square that she now called home, she had thrust the meeting with the Earl out of her mind. She had to consider the evening meal.

At her insistence, they had dispensed with the services of cooks and maids in order to free more funds for air flight. She did not mind doing household chores.

She only wished Uncle Arthur would listen to her. She wanted so much to go up, to become a female aeronaut like Madame Blanchard. When other girls were playing with dolls, she had been playing with balloons. When they were thinking of trousseaus and weddings, she was thinking of ascending into the heavens in a wicker basket. But Uncle Arthur . . .

The door opened. "If the wind is favorable, everything should go right," declared Harold, running a rough hand through his brilliant hair and unbuttoning his shabby coat.

"Just so long as it don't change after they get up," Uncle Arthur said. "You remember what happened to Sadler when he went up during the Victory Celebration in '15. Got blown off course and landed in the Mucking Marshes."

Uncle Arthur's red hair was not as vivid as his son's, and there was much less of it. But it presented a rather startling picture, curling as it did round a shiny bald pate.

"I'm sure it will go right," repeated Harold. "We've considered all the things we could."

Uncle Arthur sighed. "It's the things we can't consider that worry me. If we're ever going to get anywhere with commercial air flight, we've got to show people that it's safe and convenient. That it can actually work."

Harold scratched his peeling nose, constantly sunburned from his days outdoors. "We need a female aeronaut. To prove it ain't dangerous."

Bless Harold, he was trying his best to help her go aloft.

But Uncle Arthur just frowned. "A female's got no place in air flight. Wouldn't want one in a balloon with me."

Biting her lip, Aurelia turned back to the pot of soup she was ladling up. Why couldn't Uncle Arthur understand? Why couldn't he see that a female could be as devoted to air flight as any man?

"I want to read again about the Montgolfier flights," Uncle Arthur went on. "Even though we are using hydrogen gas instead of hot air like they did, we may find mention of something we've missed."

He looked at his son. "You have consulted your records on air currents, temperature, and pressure variations? Wind velocities, too? You know how important they are."

"Yes, father. I know. I've studied them carefully. We have all the information ready."

"Oh, if only I were going up." She was unaware she'd spoken aloud until the men turned to regard her.

"This is not a task for females." Uncle Arthur's face reddened. "It takes intelligence and judgment. A man has to make quick decisions. And right ones."

Aurelia bristled. "Do you mean to say that I have no intelligence and judgment?"

"Of course not, my dear." Uncle Arthur's tone was placating. He rubbed his bald head in that way he had when he was worried. "Aurelia, you know that I gave your father my word that I would not let you go aloft."

"But it's not fair. You know it's not fair."

Uncle Arthur sighed. "Would you have me break my word? To your poor dead father?"

Of course she didn't want that. But neither did she want to be forever denied the joy of ascent. She had more intelligence than many men. But even if she could prove that, it was no use. He had promised Papa.

But *she* hadn't promised. Somehow, some way, she was going to get up there. She meant to experience the heavens firsthand.

"You took the handbill to the printer?" Uncle Arthur asked.

"Yes." Harold gave her a commiserating look. "He promised them faithfully for Tuesday morning."

"Good. That will give us ample time to hand them out. Tell me again, how did the wording read?"

Harold closed his eyes and recited. "Thursday next, 11:00 A.M. Balloon Ascent from Hyde Park. Howard Amesley, Celebrated Aeronaut. Spectators welcome."

Uncle Arthur nodded. "Very good, my

boy. Very good indeed." He pushed back his chair. "Now to dinner."

Some time later, the remains of the meal cleared away, Aurelia retired to her room and lit the lamp. She did not join the men in their computations. They would simply figure and refigure — an exceedingly dull task.

She did not put a match to the little fire laid on the hearth, but instead pulled her shawl closer and settled down with *The Dark Stranger*. Lady Incognita's romances could always be counted on to keep one's interest. And that night she needed something to distract her mind from the intended flight and Uncle Arthur's unreasonable attitude.

She was several chapters into the book when she realized that she had been casting the hero in the likeness of a certain Lord Ranfield. From piercing eyes to broad shoulders, the dark stranger, whose name the heroine had yet to discover, was the image of the Earl. A slightly sobered Earl, perhaps, but still amazingly like.

Aurelia made a *moue* of distaste. This afternoon's adventure had been just that — an adventure and nothing more. She should not be so foolish as to refine on it.

Still, she let her eyes slowly close. Talking to him had been invigorating. Even now her blood raced at the memory. What a terribly vivid blue his eyes were. And how they could hold a woman's gaze! For several minutes she let herself imagine what might have happened.

For one thing, they might have attended the theater together. Though she'd never had a chance to attend, she'd heard about the performances at Drury Lane and Covent Garden. How the *ton* went to see each other, not the play.

She and the Earl might have ridden in Hyde Park, behind the highsteppers he no doubt kept. Or they might have waltzed at Almack's, the "wanton" waltz as Byron called it, because he said it heated the blood. And, perhaps, the gossips whispered, because his clubfoot prevented him from enjoying it himself.

She stirred uncomfortably in her chair. She didn't need a waltz to heat her blood. Just imagining a look from the Earl's heavy-lidded eyes could do that quite adequately. The thought rather shocked her.

She was a grown woman, of course, with some knowledge of the ways of the world. And she'd turned down more than one invitation to matrimony for the very reason that she could not countenance intimacy with the man who offered it, even though some of them had been likable enough. But this was a far different feeling than any she had previously experienced. And really rather strange. It made her feel . . .

She sighed. Perhaps she should put *The Dark Stranger* aside and try instead Miss Eliza Museat's book.

She was quite determined to think no more of the Earl. Consequently, she had read a great deal of Miss Museat's *Romance of the 18th Century, Altered from the Italian*, by the time she rose to prepare for bed. What a strange book it was — imagine a seventeen-year-old heroine passionately in love with a married man of fifty. Surely this was too much.

But she had to admit that these romances had considerably brightened her own dull existence. Without them, her winters would have been exceedingly drab. And no matter what their peculiarities, she did not intend to give them up.

By the time she turned out the lamp and slid between the sheets, she had made another decision. She would think no more of the Earl of Ranfield.

However, this excellent resolution proved not so easily achieved. For immediately upon the conclusion of her prayers, the image of the man intruded again upon her consciousness. With an irritated exclamation, she admitted the truth to herself. Wrong and utterly hopeless as she knew the thing to be, an idea much more fitting for a green schoolroom girl than a grown woman of sense, she very much desired to see the dark, handsome Earl again.

She knew, of course, that she would not. Her behavior that afternoon had certainly convinced him that she found his company abhorrent. She would not have the excitement of his conversation, but then neither would she be led into temptation. She sighed, actually regretting her rudeness. Never before had temptation appeared so pleasant.

Chapter

Three

The first Thursday in May dawned bright and sunny — a good day for flight. Aurelia put on her best bombazine and the bonnet with the pink rosette.

Harold, of course, wore his aeronautical attire. His scarlet coat was adorned with enough gold braid to dazzle the weariest worldly eye. And his curly-brimmed beaver sported a dashing crimson feather. Beside such splendor she felt quite the drab sparrow.

But of course his clothes were part of the spectacle. Spectators wanted to see something more than just a balloon rising into the air. They came out for a show. And Uncle Arthur meant to give them one.

As the three of them approached the balloon, the crowd began to wave and cheer. For a moment she felt that they were cheering her. But only for a moment. Then she was brought back to the sad realization that when Harold soared heavenward, she would be left behind.

The balloon strained against the mooring ropes, its red, blue, yellow, and green panels glowing in the sun. The brightly painted wicker gondola seemed small, even fragile. But she knew it was all quite safe.

A hundred times she'd heard them discuss it. How simple it was to go up. To go down. A hundred times she'd done it in her imagination.

Of course, they hadn't yet figured out a foolproof way to travel in the proper direction. To do that they had to find the right air current. And sometimes that could be difficult.

Still, none of that really mattered. They could fly. And that was above all wonderful.

"Oh, Uncle Arthur! It's quite the most marvelous thing I've ever seen."

He nodded happily, his round face glowing. "Yes, my dear. It is indeed."

They stopped beside the basket, and she reached out a tentative hand to touch it. It moved under her fingers, almost like a live thing. It wanted to go, too. To float free.

Oh, it was so grossly unfair.

"Time to load up," Harold said. He began to unpack the things they'd brought — blankets, maps, food, and water.

She forced herself to smile at him. It was

not, after all, Harold's fault that Papa had elicited that promise from Uncle Arthur. Harold would be willing — even happy — to share the heavens with her. It was Uncle Arthur who refused her that much-longed-for happiness.

"Oh, if only I could stand in it." She turned to her uncle. "Please? Just for a little while? To see what it's like? That wouldn't break your promise."

He was weakening, she could see. "Oh, very well. You may get in the basket. Harold will hand you the supplies. Pack them carefully."

"Oh yes. Thank you."

She climbed the platform and lowered herself into the gondola.

"You can help me weigh-off," Harold said.

He was smiling, and she knew he understood her excitement. "Now, release a little gas."

She pulled the rope that opened the lever.

"Just a little," Harold cautioned. "Too much and she won't rise."

The balloon quivered. It was a strange sensation — to have it moving under her feet like some living being.

He passed her a pile of blankets, and she put them along the basket's edge. They always traveled with emergency supplies. Uncle Arthur was a careful man.

She cast a longing look up at the sky. Soon Harold would be up there.

He handed her the water jugs. "I'm sorry, Reely," he whispered. "I know you want to go up."

She nodded, unable to speak. She wanted it so badly. It was horribly unfair.

Under a tree some distance away, her uncle was discussing aeronautics with two elegantly dressed gentlemen. "Harold," he called.

"Coming, Papa."

Aurelia watched them for a moment. Then she looked up at the towering balloon. It strained at the tether ropes. Oh, to go up. Just once.

But in a few minutes they would come back. They would make her get out of the gondola. And Harold would get in and sail away. Unless . . .

Her heart jumped around in her throat. Everything was already aboard. She knew exactly what to do. And she would do it. If only they didn't come back too soon.

She bent and began unfastening the tether ropes. She would prove to Uncle Arthur that she *could* be an aeronaut. And then . . . The last rope came loose, and the balloon floated upward.

It was quite unlike anything she had imagined. She stood, gripping the basket's rim, while the ground receded below her. The people, their heads tilted back, watched and cheered. They thought she was part of the act.

She heard one muttered exclamation from Uncle Arthur. But he did not call up to order her down. Perhaps he didn't want people to know something had gone wrong.

But whatever he thought, it couldn't matter. At that moment nothing mattered but the wondrous fact of being airborne.

All around her the world was growing. She could see farther and farther — and in all directions. Incredibly, the floor of the basket did not seem to move at all. Under her feet it remained firm and solid.

As Hyde Park fell away, she drew in a deep breath. Oh, the beauty of it. The peace. The serenity.

She stretched her arms wide, wanting to encompass it all. It was worth everything — anything — to have this experience at last.

But she must make the most of it. Let's see. Drop ballast to go up. Release gas to go down. She was already quite high, gloriously high.

Treetops like green carpet. And the sky —

the brilliant blue sky. Oh, it was so marvelously beautiful.

It was some minutes later before she realized that she was growing chill. Of course, she was reaching the rarefied atmosphere Uncle Arthur had mentioned.

She took a blanket from the pile and draped it, shawl-like, around her shoulders. Snuggled into it, she smiled and leaned on the basket's rim. Air flight at last.

The world unfolded itself beneath her, and Aurelia lost herself in its beauty. Twice she added blankets to the one around her shoulders. But finally the increasing cold became too much to bear. And she could no longer forget Uncle Arthur. He would be angry. But he would also be worried.

With a sigh, she pulled herself from contemplation of the lovely vista of sky and earth and began searching for that particular patch of green from which she'd ascended. She'd had her fun, and now it was time to pay the piper.

But she could not see Hyde Park. There were meadows and treetops. Winding ribbon roads and miniature houses and barns. Even little dots of people. But there was nothing that looked like Hyde Park. Nothing at all.

And then she noticed that the ground beneath was flowing by quite rapidly. The wind was bearing the balloon along, faster and faster. But in what direction?

She consulted the compass mounted on the basket's rim. Southeast — the wind was bearing her to the southeast. That way lay Dover. And beyond Dover the Channel!

"Well." She said it aloud because she longed suddenly for the sound of a human voice. "I'll just drop down and catch a current going the other way."

She pulled the rope that opened the valve to release gas. The balloon descended a little. But the air current still kept pushing it toward the Channel.

"Calm," said Aurelia to herself, in a voice that was not noticeably so. "I must be calm. If I can't get back to Hyde Park, I'll just land. Anywhere will do." And she released more gas. "It will just take a little time."

But this current, too, bore the balloon southeast. And the sky, which had been so breathtakingly blue, turned dark and threatening. A great glowering cloud blotted out the sun. And huge drops of rain began pelting down, bouncing off her bonnet, and soaking into the blankets.

Thunder rumbled and rolled above her. A flash of lightning leaping out of a cloud sent her tumbling backward. She hit the rim of the gondola and slid to the floor. For a moment she huddled there, dazed.

But then she scrambled to her feet and reached for the rope. If she could bring the balloon down safely through such a raging storm, wouldn't Uncle Arthur have to admit to her capabilities?

There! To the left. Beyond that mass of treetops. Was that a meadow? She pulled again at the rope.

The wind was growing stronger. It buffeted the big balloon from side to side, making it hard for her to keep erect.

Clinging to the basket's rim, she peered from beneath her dripping bonnet. That *was* a meadow. She yanked at the valve rope.

Suddenly, the wind took the balloon and, with a great sickening swoop, dropped it downward. Aurelia tumbled backward again. There were terrible noises — of scratching, of scraping, of snapping branches. She dragged herself to her feet in time to see that she was headed right for a huge wall.

The gondola struck another branch and tilted sideways. She lost her grip, falling heavily against the ballast. There was a terrible sickening crash, the sound of whinnying horses, and, then, blessed darkness.

★ ★ ★

She woke to find herself in a strange bed. She was oddly light-headed and the room had a curious tendency to blur, but she was alive. She tried to raise her head, but it was terribly heavy and throbbed horribly.

Her right ankle, too, must have been injured. A dull pain ate at it. Slowly, she tested her limbs, laboriously raising each of them. They, at least, were functioning.

Carefully, she raised a hand to her head, which by now was thudding dully. Her probing fingers found a large lump on her left temple. She let her arm fall back onto the coverlet. Oh dear, weak as a newborn kitten. And what had happened to the balloon? Uncle Arthur was going to be very angry. And rightly so.

The door opened, and she heard someone crossing the room. A man moved into her line of vision.

"So," observed the Earl of Ranfield with obvious satisfaction. "You're awake."

A riot of questions raced through Aurelia's mind, but she could only stare, wide-eyed.

"I suppose you're wondering what happened," he continued companionably, pulling up a delicate lyre-back chair and straddling it. Poor thing, she was obviously

53

dazed. His first suspicion was clearly unfounded. No one would deliberately engineer such a mishap, not even a fortune-struck young woman.

Besides, her appearance had solved a problem for him. Now he would not have to return to the city to seek her out.

He suppressed an urge to pat her shoulder, and an even stronger one to smooth that golden hair.

Finally she found her tongue. "The balloon? What happened to the balloon?"

"It only suffered a few tears. I shouldn't worry about it."

"Perhaps you shouldn't!" She gave him a dark look. "But balloons cost a lot of money." In her agitation she attempted to sit up, then grabbed at her head, and fell back.

"Please," he said. "Don't bedevil yourself."

But she wasn't hearing him. "I must get back to London."

He shook his head. "I'm afraid that won't be possible just yet. My physician assures me that travel is out of the question for you for some time to come."

"Oh no." She pulled herself up in the bed. More slowly this time. "Really, milord. I cannot possibly impose upon your hospitality. I must return to London."

He tried to smile encouragingly. Why didn't she believe him? "I assure you, my dear Miss Amesley, I always attend to the words of my physician, a very wise man."

"But . . ." she faltered.

She must still be in pain. Clearly she was not up to traveling.

"They will be worried about me. Harold and Uncle Arthur."

He tried to reassure her. "I have thought of that very contingency. In fact, I dispatched a rider to tell Harold that you're here."

She was looking quite pale. "Here," he said, getting to his feet. "Let me help you to lie down. You don't want to take a chill."

And then she looked down and realized that she was wearing only a nightdress. With a gasp she slid downward, clutching the coverlet. How refreshing her innocence was.

He reseated himself. "How fortunate that you and Phoebe are of a size."

She stared at him. "Phoebe?"

"Yes," he explained. "It is her nightdress that you are wearing. Phoebe is Cousin Prudence's daughter." He smiled at her again. "Several years ago Cousin Prudence was widowed. And, since I needed someone to manage my household, she came here. And Phoebe with her."

Aurelia nodded. Her head seemed all fuzzy. Thoughts wandered around, bumping into each other like pedestrians in a London fog. But always her thoughts kept coming back to one thing — Uncle Arthur and their balloon.

"How did I come down? That is, did I do much damage?"

The Earl shook his head. "Not much. The gondola skimmed the tops off some trees. Then it crashed into my stable."

"The horses! They weren't injured?"

"No, no. Nothing was injured but yourself. Your ankle appears to be sprained. My physician says you must keep off it for several days. Also, you suffered a blow on the head when you fell against the sandbags. Dr. Monkton feels certain no concussion occurred, but still recommends bed rest. So you see," he continued. "The prescription is a double one."

Aurelia nodded. He was right, of course. She had no conveyance in which to return to London. There was the balloon to think of. And beyond that, she did not know that she would be able to undertake such a journey. The room was having a disconcerting tendency to blur around the edges.

His eyes held hers. "Think of this as your home until you are well again," he said. His gaze turned critical. "It looks to me as if you are tiring. I believe you had better rest now. We will talk later."

Rising from the chair, he again advanced to the bed. "Let me fluff up your pillows."

He was so kind, so understanding. Why must her heart jump about in her breast like that?

One strong hand slid behind her to support her shoulders, while with the other he plumped up the pillows. She felt his hand through the thin gown, warm and comforting. Her face was only an inch from his waistcoat and she inhaled the male smell of him — leather and soap and a hint of pomade. It made her head whirl even more dizzily.

He laid her carefully back, then adjusted the covers around her neck. She felt the merest touch of his fingers beneath her chin. Then, smiling, he reached up to push back a damp curl on her forehead.

"You must listen to me. You are in for a nice rest whether you wish it or not." He straightened and eyed her with mock severity. "Females have no call to be wafted about in balloons, you know. Dangerous business that. If I were your uncle, I should forbid it absolutely."

"My uncle . . ." But she was too tired to go into all that. "Air flight is perfectly safe. And if males can do it, why not females?"

"Why not indeed?" he agreed, his eyebrow rising.

She suspected his agreement was meant to be ironic, but her eyelids were so heavy. A sweet lethargy was creeping over her, and, finally, she let the soft darkness carry her away.

Chapter

Four

Aurelia slept soundly for some twelve hours. When she woke, the throbbing in her head was gone. That, at least, was a blessing. A dull ache in the vicinity of her ankle informed her that the injury there had been more severe.

Still, the morning sun coming through the windowpanes played in golden rays on the silken coverlet, and outside the sparrows chirped happily. It looked like a beautiful spring day.

She was leaning slightly to one side, in an effort to see more of the room than was clearly visible through the blue brocade curtains of the bed, when the door opened.

"Good morning," said the pleasant round-faced woman whose spectacles looked in danger of sliding off the tip of her almost nonexistent nose. "I'm Mrs. Esterhill — Cousin Prudence. And I've brought you some food."

Aurelia pushed herself to an upright position. "Thank you. A roll and some chocolate would be most welcome."

Mrs. Esterhill snorted, a delicate sound yet plainly expressing her opinion of such foolishness. "You'll not be having such a mishmash as that. Not in any household I have the running of. I've brought you a decent meal. Eggs, bacon, sausages, toast, rolls, marmalade. And a good pot of hot tea."

"Oh, how lovely!"

Mrs. Esterhill beamed. "You're a nice child, you are. Proper brought up. Now my Phoebe . . ."

"Now, Mama," said a young woman from the doorway.

Phoebe Esterhill was dark-eyed like her Mama. But there the resemblance ended. For where Mrs. Esterhill was round, Phoebe was slender. And the mother's hair, though dark as the daughter's, was salted with gray.

Phoebe crossed the room. "I'm pleased to meet you," she said. "We don't get many visitors."

"And certain none falling from the skies!"

"Now, Mama."

"Don't you now Mama me," said Cousin Prudence. "This young woman is fortunate to be alive. Up there in that Devil's contrivance. It's unnatural. That's what it is." She turned to Aurelia. "Whatever could your Papa be thinking of? Letting you go into such danger."

"Now, Mama. Let the poor thing eat."

Cousin Prudence made a face. "I'll be back later," she said, bustling out.

"You must forgive Mama." Phoebe's expression was earnest. "She means well. Go ahead, do eat."

The food looked delicious. Aurelia set to with a will.

Phoebe kept silent till the last bite had disappeared. And then she said, "Oh, do tell me. What was it like? Up there in the heavens?"

Aurelia smiled. "No words can describe it. My cousin Harold, he's an aeronaut. He says he never feels so good as when he's up there. Above everything."

"Oh yes. It sounds simply marvelous. Ever since Cousin Ranfield mentioned it, I have wanted to go aloft." She frowned. "But Mama won't let me."

Aurelia felt an instant kinship. "I know just what you mean. Uncle Arthur would not let me go up. Some people are quite silly about these things."

Phoebe's dark eyes grew wide. "Then how . . ."

"It rather just happened." Thinking back, she felt a distinct sense of embarrassment. "You see, Harold was supposed to go up. From Hyde Park. Uncle Arthur said I might watch."

She found herself clutching Phoebe's hand. "I wanted to go up. So much. I begged him to let me just stand in the gondola. I thought that would make me feel better."

She swallowed. This was the hard part of the story. "While I was in there, Harold said everything was ready. But then Uncle Arthur called to him. And he went over to talk. And . . . And I just cast off."

Phoebe laughed and clapped her hands. "Oh, I quite understand. You could not pass up such a marvelous opportunity."

"Yes. And up I went."

"Oh, how romantic. It's like something from Lady Incognita."

Aurelia stared. "Lady Incognita? You read Lady Incognita?"

"Read?" Phoebe declared. "I positively pore over her. I have every book she's ever written. Two or three copies of some."

Aurelia smiled. "I think she's quite the best of writers."

Phoebe reached out to touch her arm. "Oh, I am so glad you're here. Not glad

62

you've fallen, of course. But glad that if you must fall . . . Oh, you know what I mean."

"Yes, I do. And I feel the same. How rare to have found a friend that enjoys reading romances. Uncle Arthur and Harold have no use for anything but balloon flight." Aurelia took a sip of tea. "I think of it, too, of course. But not all the time."

"So you went up," Phoebe said, obviously eager to hear more of the adventure. "Then what happened?"

"At first it was delightful. I could see so far. I quite lost myself in contemplating it. So much so that for some time I didn't realize that the air current was taking me away from Hyde Park. Finally, I dropped down to find one that would take me back. But I simply could not."

Phoebe shivered. "And then you were swept into the thunderstorm. Oh, how deliciously frightening."

Aurelia considered this. "Well, I did feel some fear. But it wasn't particularly delicious. Most of the time I was too busy to be afraid. However, I did everything I should have." She sighed. "Uncle Arthur will not believe that. He will call it female unintelligence."

In the doorway Ranfield cleared his throat. The two of them, sitting so close, looked like little girls getting ready to do mischief.

"Perhaps your uncle would be right," he said as they looked up.

Miss Amesley shook her head. "No, he would not. I am well versed in ballooning techniques. I know exactly what to do to go where I wish."

With some difficulty he kept himself from chuckling. What a plucky little thing she was. "Then am I to infer that you wished to go crashing into my stable?"

"Of course not. That was the result of the storm."

She and Phoebe exchanged looks. They were bosom bows already, it seemed.

He shook his head. "A woman, aloft in a balloon. And alone. What was your uncle thinking of?"

"Oh," Phoebe blurted out, "her uncle didn't know."

From the look of dismay on her face, this was not a piece of intelligence Miss Amesley wished him to have.

Still, he could not resist pursuing the question. And soon Phoebe, who had never been able to withstand his look of command, had divulged the whole story.

"So you stole your uncle's balloon."

Miss Amesley bristled like a hedgehog

and sent him a fulminating look. "Indeed, I did not. That balloon is as much mine as it is his."

He felt a pang of remorse. What was he doing, baiting this innocent just because he liked to see her reactions? That was hardly a gentlemanly thing to do.

"I see. Well, enough about air flight for now." He turned to Phoebe. "Please call a maid. And, if you will, get Miss Amesley one of your gowns. I want to show her around."

"But my ankle . . ."

He smiled. "I have the perfect means to convey you."

"But . . ."

"I'll be back in half an hour."

"She'll be ready," Phoebe said.

And ready she was. In a gown of pale lavender, with a high neck edged in lace, a smocked bodice, and long sleeves trimmed with brown velvet ribbon, she lay on the chaise, feeling quite the lady.

And he was on time. "So, all ready."

"Yes, but . . ."

"No buts. I'm taking you out to the garden for a breath of fresh air." He bent to her. "Now, it would be most helpful if you'd put your arms around my neck."

"My arms?" He couldn't mean . . .

"I mean put your arms around my neck."

She did so with some misgiving. His arms were very strong. She felt completely safe there. That is, she amended, she felt he would not drop her.

But these other feelings were hard to analyze — excitement and breathlessness. And a weakness that, had she been otherwise capable of standing, would still have left her clinging to him for support.

He carried her easily down the great stairs and out the front door. "This is my park," he said. "All laid out with due respect to Nature, by the late Capability Brown."

Raising her head, she saw a vast rolling expanse of land, dotted with clumps of scattered trees. "How lovely," she murmured.

"Over there," he continued, "are my stables. Rather nice ones, if I may say so." He grinned. "At least before they were assaulted by your balloon."

Aurelia looked up into the dark face so close to her own. He was certainly the handsomest man. "I'm truly sorry about that. Uncle Arthur will make reparations."

"Nonsense. I was bamming you. The horses were not hurt. Nor the stables. So all is well."

Moving off toward the rear of the great

rambling house, he came to a bench set under a flowering tree. There he gently deposited her.

To avoid the riot of thoughts caused by his nearness, she concentrated on the house — a great boxlike shape of red brick, now mellowed to a soft dull pink.

He settled himself beside her. "The center of the house was built by the first Earl in the seventeenth century. Fifty years later the third Earl added the wing to your right, now housing the kitchens. And forty years after that, the fourth built the wing to your left." He smiled at her. "He was quite a sociable sort. Things were lively then."

His voice hardened. "My own father had no time for such pursuits. He cared only to acquire, not to enjoy, his possessions."

Aurelia indicated the flourishing flowers. "And all this?"

A smile of tenderness lit his face. "This was my mother's doing. Mother was a proponent of her own school of gardening. She thought Brown, or Repton, or even la Nôtre, too rigid for her taste. She simply did as she pleased. Since she did not enjoy city life, in her later years she lived at Ranfield winter and summer. These gardens were her particular delight."

His eyes clouded. "I remember her sitting

on this very bench, feeding the tame squirrels."

He smiled. "It was rather hard work for a young lad with his first gun not to be tempted by such largess. But I took care to do my shooting far from Mother's beloved garden."

He sighed. "I'm afraid my neighbors must think me odd. I never join the hunt now. Haven't the heart for it since she died."

He started, as though realizing the unusual nature of his revelations. "You must excuse me. I don't know what possessed me to rattle on like that. I don't usually bore my guests with such tales."

She did not know how to respond. Certainly it was not boredom she was feeling. But it would not be proper to tell him that. Instead, she took a deep breath. "Are we close to the sea?"

"Why do you ask?"

She managed a small smile. "I think perhaps I can smell it."

"It's quite possible that you can. When the wind is right, the breeze can be salty. After your ankle's better, we'll go exploring. There are some interesting caves among the cliffs."

"That sounds very enjoyable."

Ranfield discovered an intriguing dimple

on her chin. He liked the way she was smiling at him, too. What was there about her smile that made his heart a little lighter, the world a little brighter?

"But," she continued, "Uncle Arthur will be coming. And Harold. We shall be returning to London."

The thought was not a happy one. He pushed it aside. "You cannot leave till you are fully recovered. That will take some time."

"The other day," she went on, without any of those distracting looks and fluttering eyelashes affected by *tonnish* ladies, "I neglected to ask if you have been up in a balloon."

"Once," he said. "In Paris."

"Paris!"

"Yes. I was there for a while after the campaign in Spain. And I saw some military balloons. Observation ones."

Her eyes lit up as another woman's might at the mention of diamonds. "Were they *montgolfières* or *charlières?*"

"I beg your pardon?"

"Were they propelled by hot air or hydrogen gas?"

For a moment, engrossed by her fresh beauty, he forgot to answer.

"Milord?" she persisted. "Hot air or gas?"

He sighed. "I'm afraid I don't know." The chit was making him feel decidedly ignorant.

"Was there a brazier suspended beneath the balloon?"

He tried to remember. If she wanted to talk about balloons, he would do his best to please her. "There may have been. I can not recollect."

She frowned, her forehead wrinkling in concentration. He wanted to reach out, to smooth the lines away. To touch her soft cheek . . .

"It's probable they were *montgolfières*. Hot airs are cheaper to maintain."

Her voice was soft, too, delightfully soft. "Yes, I suppose so."

"You see . . ." And off she went into a disquisition on the relative merits of hydrogen gas and hot air, *charlières* versus *montgolfières*. He heard very little of it, actually, because her sparkling eyes, her animated face, and that kissable pink mouth kept driving his thoughts in quite another direction.

Finally, she drew to a close. "So you see, though hydrogen is costlier, it is probably safer."

"Yes, I see."

She lapsed into silence then, gazing over the blossoming flowers. She was like a flower herself — a tender new bud just beginning to open.

But then common sense reared its head — and insisted that there was too much coincidence here. Could they — she and Harold — have contrived this so-called accident? Could this simply be the case of another young woman looking to catch a rich husband?

He considered the ramifications of this unpleasant possibility with some thoroughness. It was possible. But it certainly didn't seem probable. How could they have predicted a thunderstorm? And that story of how she'd gotten around her uncle's edict against going up — knowing her as he did now, that seemed so likely.

And there was something else to consider. He was no stranger to female tricks. He'd been exposed to the whole battery — and more than once. But with her there were no fluttering eyelashes or coy looks. No tinkling laughter or accidental brushing of hand against hand. Indeed, she'd been — or at least seemed — quite disconcerted by his carrying her about like that. Too bad, for he had found it most enjoyable.

He experienced a twinge of guilt. How could he be suspecting such an innocent? And she not even recovered from the effects of the crash. Was this excursion outdoors too much for her? Had he let his desire for her conversation override his instincts to protect her?

He considered her face, soft and relaxed as she took in the beauty of the flowers. He intended to look for signs of weariness, but soon he was just enjoying the sight of her.

"Milord?" she asked finally, hesitantly, putting a hand to her cheek.

"Yes, Miss Amesley?"

"Why do you stare at me so? Have I perhaps some other injury?"

"No, no." He hastened to reassure her. "I am just looking to see if you're fatigued."

She sighed, a little wisp of sound that made him want to take her in his arms, to shield her, to keep her safe forever. And then she turned those great dark eyes on him. "You're very kind. I am feeling just a trifle fatigued."

"Then I shall return you to your room." He wanted more of her companionship. But her comfort was of more importance than his wants. So, before he could talk himself out of it, he gathered her up and went striding off toward the house.

Aurelia found her heart beginning to pound. She tried to calm the silly thing. After all, he had carried her before. But with her arms wrapped around his neck and her cheek resting against his waistcoat, she could feel the beating of his heart, a heart that seemed to throb in rhythm with her own.

So by the time they reached her room, she knew her cheeks were quite pinker and her breath quite faster than they should be.

He put her carefully on the bed and smiled down at her. "Perhaps a nap would be in order before dinner."

"Yes." Now why had she said that? She was not feeling the least bit tired. She'd only come back to her room because he suggested it.

She felt his touch, featherlight, as he smoothed back a curl on her forehead. And then he was gone.

The minute the door closed behind him she regretted her acquiescence. Here she was, wide awake and full of energy — and forced to lie abed like some invalid. It was quite annoying.

Chapter

Five

Aurelia was still annoyed a long time later when a slight creaking sound turned her attention to the door. It opened very slowly and Phoebe peered around it.

"Oh, do come in!" Aurelia cried. "Please. I am quite beside myself with boredom."

Phoebe advanced to the bed. "Perhaps I should not bother you. Ranfield said you were sleeping."

Aurelia shook her head. "He suggested that I nap, but I could not. I have already rested for so long." She picked at the coverlet. "I am not used to doing nothing."

Phoebe nodded. "I suspected as much. So I brought you some books to read."

Aurelia took the proffered volumes. "*The Dark Stranger*. Oh, thank you. And a new book. *Frankenstein* by Mary Shelley. I hope I have time to finish it before I must leave."

"Leave!" Phoebe's face reflected alarm. "You cannot leave!"

Aurelia smiled sadly. "Phoebe, I'm afraid

I must. Uncle Arthur and Harold will be coming for me. We'll have to return to London."

Phoebe dragged a zebrawood chair to the bed. "I don't believe you shall be returning to the city."

"You don't?"

Lowering her voice, Phoebe looked rather anxiously toward the door. "You see, you are the answer to my prayers."

"I am? Why?"

Phoebe's forehead wrinkled. "I have been so dreadfully lonely here. Mama reads nothing but Scripture. Why, if it were not for Ranfield's library, I should have long ago gone mad."

At the mention of his name, Aurelia felt herself coloring. What an extraordinary effect the man had on her.

"His lordship buys romances for you?" she asked.

Phoebe nodded, her eyes again on the door. "He tells Mama they are for him. She can't disapprove of *him*, of course. And he does read them sometimes. I know — for we talk about them."

The prospect of daily discussion with the Earl, and over such an interesting topic, left Aurelia wishing herself in Phoebe's slippers. She heaved a giant sigh. "That must be quite interesting."

"It is." Phoebe's eyes took on a speculative light. "What do you think of Ranfield?"

"I . . . He . . ." Aurelia found it difficult to go on. Thinking about the Earl made her heart behave in a most peculiar fashion. Speaking about him was even more difficult.

Phoebe smiled. "Aurelia, you aren't . . . You haven't . . . That is, could you possibly have conceived a *tendre* for Ranfield?"

The question left Aurelia almost as breathless as the Earl did. "A *tendre?* For Ranfield? I truly don't know."

The two looked at each other.

Aurelia sighed again. "I have been feeling most peculiar lately."

Phoebe considered this. "Since your accident?"

"Well, actually since that day in the park."

Phoebe's mouth fell open. "What day in the park? Oh, do tell me."

"The day Harold introduced me to his lordship."

Phoebe pleated the material of her gown and looked thoughtful. "And has your heart been palpitating?"

Aurelia frowned. "Hearts do not really palpi— Oh, Phoebe, they do! At least, mine does. Do you really think . . . ?"

Phoebe nodded. "I'm afraid it sounds suspiciously like love."

Aurelia's heart gave several lively jumps. "Love? But Phoebe, I know nothing of love."

Phoebe's sigh echoed through the room. "Nor I. But oh, I should like to. I should very much like to." She clasped Aurelia's hand. "Just think, when you and Ranfield marry, we shall be cousins."

"M-marry?" Aurelia repeated. "But surely if his lordship wanted a wife, he would have chosen one by now."

Phoebe looked thoughtful. "He's three and thirty. He's had plenty of time."

"Then perhaps he does not mean to marry."

Phoebe raised an eyebrow. "Impossible. He must marry and provide an heir."

"Still . . ."

"No." Phoebe smiled. "It's actually quite obvious. The man needs a wife."

"But . . ."

"No 'buts,' " said Phoebe, in a tone so like Ranfield's that Aurelia dissolved into laughter.

When she could speak again, she shook her head. "Phoebe, we should not build dream castles like this."

"And why not?"

"Well, dream castles are so unreal. After

all, we have no indication that his lord-ship . . ." She faltered. "That is, he has been most kind, but perhaps he has a liking in an-other direction."

Phoebe considered this. "I think not. He has made no mention of hanging out for a wife."

Aurelia bethought herself of the Earl's meeting with Alvanley. "Is there someone named Annette?"

Phoebe shook her head. "I know no one of that name. Ranfield wouldn't marry without telling us."

"But Phoebe, dear, you still forget. I'll be going back to London."

Phoebe shook her head. "You must not. You must stay and marry Ranfield. Oh, Aurelia, it will be above all marvelous. You and I deal so famously together al-ready."

"Yes, we do. But isn't it more impor-tant . . . ? That is, shouldn't the Earl and I . . . ?"

"Shouldn't the Earl and you what?" came his voice from the doorway.

Aurelia jumped, feeling the blood rush to her cheeks. Her mind went a perfect blank. "I . . ." His coming in so unexpectedly had cast her into a regular flutter. She could not think. She could not speak. She could scarcely breathe. But she did have enough presence of mind to look at Phoebe.

And, blessedly, Phoebe sprang into the breach. "Shouldn't Aurelia and you talk about ballooning," she explained.

How resourceful Phoebe was. Aurelia felt her wits returning. "Yes," she said. "I was afraid that perhaps I had bent your ear too much. Earlier when we were discussing air flight."

"Of course you did not." The Earl advanced into the room. "As I told you, I am much interested in ballooning."

What a fine figure of a man he made. His coat fit so smoothly across his shoulders, his fawn inexpressibles showed not a single wrinkle, and his Wellingtons gleamed in the spring sun.

Her heart *was* palpitating. Could Phoebe be right? Could these strange feelings mean that she had, at last, met a man who could make her think seriously of matrimony?

The thought was disconcerting, especially with him standing right there, bigger than life. And oh so handsome.

"I came to check on you. To see if you were still resting. But since I find you awake, I'll just leave you to Phoebe's company till dinner."

He surveyed her carefully. "You're

looking rather flushed," he remarked. "Are you sure you're not coming down with a fever?"

"Oh no, milord. I feel quite well."

She could hardly tell him that her high color was the direct result of his presence. But she was quite certain he was the cause.

He came toward the bed and put a hand to her forehead. His touch was gentle, tender. Like a mother's. Except that no mother's touch had ever set a heart to such insane fluttering.

"No," he said thoughtfully. "You don't feel feverish."

He turned to Phoebe. "If she seems tired, you will see that she rests."

"Of course."

"Then I'll see you both at dinner."

Aurelia stared after his departing figure, her mind a veritable chaos of thoughts.

There was silence for several moments after his departure. Then Phoebe turned back to the bed. "Well?"

"I . . . I think perhaps you are right. I seem to have conceived a partiality for the Earl."

Phoebe's smile was ecstatic. "Oh, this is so romantic."

Aurelia was still not convinced. "But Phoebe dear, these are *my* feelings. Not his lordship's."

Phoebe shook her head. "Oh, but I saw how he looked at you! With longing in his eyes. Just like the dark stranger looked at Corrinne."

A modicum of sense still remained to Aurelia, but it was being rapidly reduced by visions of herself on Ranfield's arm. Still, she tried hard to be sensible. "He has only been kind to me."

"Kind!" Phoebe's snort was very like her mother's. "Kind needn't include carrying you about like that. Or checking your forehead for a fever."

"Phoebe!"

"It's plain as the nose on your face," Phoebe declared. "He's taken with you."

Aurelia sighed. "Oh, if only that were true." To be wife to Ranfield — the picture was so enchanting she lost herself in it.

But she was not a green girl. Common sense had not entirely deserted her. "Oh, Phoebe, it simply won't wash. Your cousin is merely being kind. He has no romantic interest in me."

Phoebe frowned. "Then we shall see that he does."

"We shall?"

"Of course."

Aurelia frowned. "But Phoebe, I thought . . . That is, shouldn't the woman

81

wait for the man to fix his interest on her?"

Phoebe frowned and went to pleating her gown again. "Perhaps. But what if he doesn't?"

"I don't know. I know nothing of dangling after men. And as you said, you are equally ignorant."

"I know." Absently, Phoebe picked up the copy of *The Dark Stranger* and tapped it impatiently against her palm. "How to do it?" she mused. "How to . . . ?"

And then, looking down, she smiled. "Aurelia! That's it. It's all here!"

The quick succession of emotions had left Aurelia bewildered. Could it have also affected her ability to comprehend? "I don't understand."

"It's all here!" Phoebe repeated. "In Lady Incognita's book. Aurelia, think. Doesn't the dark stranger fall in love with Corrinne?"

"Yes, of course."

"Well, we'll just see how she did it. And then we'll do the same."

"But Phoebe, *The Dark Stranger* is not life."

"But did it not strike you as so real . . . ?"

"Yes, but we have no ruined abbeys, no ghosts, no . . . And besides, Uncle Arthur will be coming."

Phoebe frowned. "Do you want Ranfield

to dangle after you or do you not?" she demanded.

In the face of such a question Aurelia could only breathe a heartfelt, "Oh, yes, I do."

"Then we must use what we have. And what we have is *The Dark Stranger*." Phoebe smiled. "We'll find a way to keep you here."

"But . . ." Phoebe's reasoning seemed faulty, somehow. Still, she was so insistent. And perhaps . . . Who was to say that she was wrong? "All right," Aurelia agreed, finally capitulating.

Phoebe shoved the book into her hands. "Here. Read. When we come upon something that brought them together, we'll mark it."

Her eyes glittered. "We'll write it all out. We'll make it work."

Part of Aurelia still objected, but it was a small part, and growing smaller. She opened the book and began to read. "A dark cloud covered the face of the gibbous moon as though to hide from mankind's shocked sight the heinous deeds about to be perpetrated. Corrinne's tender heart quivered . . ."

Downstairs in his library, the Earl of Ranfield relaxed in a rosewood chair. His long legs stretched out in front of him, he contemplated the Turner landscape over the mantel. But he did not really see its brilliant recreations of sunlight and storm.

Those two upstairs had not been talking about ballooning when he chanced into the room. That little quiver of Phoebe's bottom lip had always signaled falsehood. But what *had* they been discussing? And how had they so quickly become close?

He sighed. Better to ask some questions he could answer. Questions of himself. Why, for instance, had the coming of Aurelia Amesley made such a difference in his life? It had been a reasonably content life — besides the work of his estate, he'd had the theater, the balls, the pretty ladies — dark willowy ladies with classic features. And life had been pleasant with all its little fripperies. Of course, he hadn't considered them fripperies, then. Before Aurelia Amesley came along, disturbing everything.

She was such a sobersides, so serious-minded. Always thinking about air flight. She was short and fair, and her features, though pleasant enough, were far from classic. She didn't flatter him. Or coo at him. Or practice any of the feminine arts on him. In sober fact she treated him exactly as she did her cousin. Or her uncle. Why then did having her around make him feel younger, smarter, happier . . . ?

He muttered a curse. He'd better find out. And soon. His messenger would have reached London by now. And, unless he much missed his guess, Harold and his father would shortly be arriving at the estate.

They would load up their beloved balloon, put Aurelia and her injured ankle in a carriage, and make a rapid return to London. And he would be left behind — a most unhappy man.

He leapt to his feet and began pacing the patterned Persian rug. Obviously, the return trip to London must be delayed. He couldn't let her go back there — not yet. Not until he had discovered . . .

Discovered what? He'd only known the chit a few days. She was a merchant's daughter, not of the *ton,* ill equipped to live in it. Even more ill equipped than Mama had been. She was not a proper wife for an earl. Not at all.

Muttering another choice expression, he kicked the fireplace fender. Damnation! What did he care about the likes and dislikes of the *ton?* About what was proper? He'd always done as he pleased. And if he ever actually contemplated getting leg-shackled, it would be to a woman he could countenance living with — and loving. What the *ton* said didn't matter.

He turned and paced the other direction. Wasn't he a man of some intelligence? Why then, he would find a way to keep them in Dover. At least until he had discovered whether or not Aurelia Amesley was the one.

He smiled and turned toward the door. The place to start was the balloon. He would go have a look at it.

Chapter

Six

By Sunday afternoon the inhabitants of the Dover estate had each made plans for the future. Cousin Prudence had marshaled a vast array of Scripture explicitly designed to point out to Aurelia Amesley the error of her ways in regard to air flight and was waiting only for the opportune moment to launch her campaign.

The Earl, having put his mind to the task at hand, had spent the previous day supervising the cleaning and refurbishing of an old shed and sending out messengers in sundry directions.

And Aurelia and Phoebe, their quills busily scratching, had read and reread *The Dark Stranger* and were making lists and more lists.

"So," said Phoebe as Aurelia reclined on her bed after their late nuncheon. "The Plan is ready. Now all we have to do is put it in motion."

Aurelia nodded. Her previous anxieties

had been forgotten in the furor of their preparations. Now she was committed, completely and irrevocably, to The Plan.

They spoke of it that way — with capital letters and in hoarse whispers — as though to say the words aloud would immediately bring them to Ranfield's ears. If only they had time to consummate it.

"So, the first thing . . ." Phoebe consulted her list, "is a runaway horse."

"Yes. I do not ride, but . . ."

"Don't tell him that," Phoebe warned. "He'll never let you on a horse at all."

"I know. But how shall I contrive it?" She turned to Phoebe. "Do you ride?"

"Only a little." Phoebe laughed. "But you must convince him that you're a better rider than I am."

"Why?"

"Because he always gives me old Strawberry. And nothing could make that horse run away."

Aurelia nodded. "Then I must ask for a more spirited animal. Is it difficult, riding?"

"Oh no, it's great fun. What I should like is a real rousing gallop — on a horse like Ranfield's mare. But he won't let me up on her."

A brisk knock sounded on the door they

had taken to keeping closed since the inception of The Plan.

"Come in," Aurelia called.

Cousin Prudence entered. "The Earl will be coming up shortly," she reported. "He means to carry you to the library. Says he has acquired a new book he wants to show you."

Aurelia and Phoebe exchanged glances. Perhaps a new romance would tell them more about how to proceed.

Cousin Prudence snorted and pushed her spectacles back up her nose. She fixed her daughter with a baleful eye. "I hope the man has not brought another of those dreadful volumes into this house. They will degrade your pure characters."

Aurelia swallowed a laugh and kept her eyes away from Mary Shelley's *Frankenstein* where it lay upon the table. Cousin Prudence would definitely not find the story of a man created from parts of the dead appropriate for their pure characters.

"Now, Mama," Phoebe said, giving that worthy personage a sweet smile. "We attended chapel this morning. We cannot read Scripture all the time, you know."

Cousin Prudence snorted again. "Perhaps not. But you could read it a great deal more than you do." And she bustled out.

Phoebe shook her head. "Poor Mama. I think she would prefer a pasty-faced hymn-singer for a daughter rather than me."

Aurelia laughed. "But I should not want you to be like that. I like you just the way you are." She smoothed the gown of blue sarcenet that Phoebe had chosen for her because it set off her hair. Would Ranfield notice it? Would he . . . ?

"Your servant has arrived," he said from the doorway. Her heart underwent a series of severe palpitations before it settled down to a more regular, if rapid, rhythm.

By now she should have been accustomed to being carried about. Indeed, her arms went quite automatically to clasp around his neck and her cheek to lie against his waistcoat. But then her heart started taking silly notions again.

Fortunately, Phoebe was there to ask, "What's the new book about, milord? We're reading Mrs. Shelley's now. It's most horrendously frightening."

"I am sorry to disappoint you, cousin." Ranfield sent Phoebe a smile that made Aurelia's heart flop over completely. "This book isn't a romance. This is a volume on aeronautics. I want to discuss it with Miss Amesley."

"Oh." Phoebe was trying to look disappointed and not being particularly successful. Wouldn't the Earl wonder why his cousin had that gleam in her eye?

"You have decided to pursue your interest in air flight then?" Aurelia tried to ask the question without letting him hear the breathlessness that was afflicting her.

"Yes," he said, looking down into her face. "But let us wait till we have reached the library."

His smile did such strange things to her — made her bones all wishy-washy and set her mind to whirling. Did that mean her partiality for him was growing stronger?

Minutes later she was carefully ensconced on a comfortable divan in front of the fire. The Earl arranged pillows behind her back and under her injured limb until she felt quite pampered — and quite breathless from his proximity.

Ranfield considered his guest. She looked comfortable. So he drew up a rosewood chair and brought her the volume from a nearby table. He wanted to talk. Air flight was interesting. But most of all he wanted to be near her. "This is about the Montgolfier brothers. Do you recommend it?"

She glanced at the title. "Yes, it is quite informational."

She was such a businesslike little thing.

So straightforward. And yet so appealing, so feminine.

"Good," he said. "Because I mean to build a balloon."

She stared at him. "You mean to build . . . ?"

"Precisely. A balloon."

Those dark eyes widened. "But . . . From a book?"

"Yes. Though actually I was hoping for some help. From you and your family."

Hoping and praying. He watched her face closely. Surely she would give him some sign of her feelings. A tender little smile, perhaps. But her features showed only surprise.

So he went on. "I calculate your family should be arriving soon. And I want your help in persuading them to stay on for a while."

Across the room Phoebe developed a sudden fit of coughing. Now what was the chit up to? But he had no time to puzzle over her behavior. He wanted Miss Amesley to stay.

"Will you help me?" he asked.

"They . . . They will want to repair our balloon."

Why did she offer excuses? Didn't she want to remain? "They can do that here."

"They will be scheduling more ascensions. You know we can go up only during warm weather."

He countered that. "I have a capital meadow. Just right for such things."

"They may need supplies — for repairs."

"I shall send my men for them."

She was silent then. Could she think of no more excuses? Did she care about him at all?

Pratt appeared in the doorway. "Visitors, milord. Mr. Arthur Amesley. Mr. Harold Amesley."

Aurelia sighed and leaned back on her pillows. Actually, she would like to sink right into them and disappear. The events of the past few days had almost driven from her mind the fact that she had made off with the balloon. And that she had caused her uncle and cousin a great deal of trouble. Uncle Arthur had every right to be angry.

"Aurelia, my dear." He hurried directly to her, his round face creased with worry. "Are you injured badly?"

"No, no, uncle. Really, I am not. I am so sorry for what I did. I cannot tell you why I did it. I just had to go up. I'm so dreadfully sorry to have caused you so much trouble . . ."

"Yes." Uncle Arthur frowned. "We were

very worried. We scoured the countryside. But then the Earl's message came." He turned. "Thank you for that, milord. It greatly relieved our minds."

Aurelia admired the ease with which his lordship handled things. "Do sit down," he said. "You must be tired after your journey."

Uncle Arthur sank into a chair. "It was fatiguing. But from worry more than anything else. I am relieved to see Aurelia looking so well."

He sighed and she felt a pang of guilt. To have made him worry so . . .

He turned to Ranfield. "The balloon . . . What happened to the balloon?"

"There is no cause for alarm there either," said the Earl. "It suffered a few tears. The gondola was scratched. Not badly."

"Good. Then we'll load it up and start back."

Aurelia's heart threatened to climb out of her chest. They mustn't . . . They couldn't . . .

The Earl smiled, the smile of one man to another. "You must not think of leaving so soon. Not after such a long journey."

"But . . ."

"Wait, please. I've something I want to

discuss with you and Harold."

"Harold? Harold!"

"Yes, Papa?"

"Come here, son. The Earl wants to talk to us."

Harold crossed the room, reluctantly, his gaze lingering on Phoebe's flushed face. And Phoebe . . .

Aurelia caught her breath. Her new friend looked even more dazed than Harold and was staring after him as though she had seen a dream come to life before her very eyes.

Aurelia shifted her attention back to the Earl. He had to persuade Uncle Arthur to stay. With Phoebe looking at Harold that way it was more imperative than ever.

"So," the Earl was saying. "I plan to assemble a *montgolfière* — a hot-air balloon. And I thought perhaps you could stay on and help me with it."

Uncle Arthur looked thoughtful. He rubbed his bald pate.

"You can repair your equipment here," his lordship continued. "I have quite a nice meadow where we can go up."

He looked toward her and Aurelia caught her breath.

"It would be a beneficial arrangement for both of us," he concluded.

Aurelia put her tongue between her teeth.

She wanted to overwhelm Uncle Arthur with reasons to stay in Dover. But, considering the trouble she'd caused him already, he wasn't likely to heed her advice. So she must keep her peace. And anxiously wait.

"Well, Harold?" his lordship asked.

Harold started. "Ah, sorry, Ranny. Wasn't listening, I'm afraid."

The Earl smiled. "I asked what you think about staying here for a while?"

"Capital idea!"

Harold beamed. She had never seen him look so happy, except, perhaps, when the new balloon arrived.

He pulled his gaze away from Phoebe again. "That is . . . I think that's a fine arrangement."

Ranfield smiled. "Good. I'll . . ."

Cousin Prudence chose that moment to bustle in. "Pratt says . . ."

"We have some guests," the Earl interjected. "They'll be staying on indefinitely."

Cousin Prudence looked the newcomers over, her eyes steely behind her spectacles. Then she fixed a blistering gaze on Uncle Arthur. "You, sir! Why ever did you let this dear child go up in that Devil's contrivance? It's inhuman, it is."

Uncle Arthur looked stunned, but he rallied quickly and leaped to his feet.

"Madame," he said, the hair around his bald pate bristling. "You accuse me unjustly. First, my niece took off against my express wishes. And second, my balloon is *not* the Devil's invention. It is the newest in scientific advancement."

Cousin Prudence straightened her cap. "Scientific advancement, is it? No one will ever convince *me* that the good Lord intended for people to fly. Look," she cried, pulling Phoebe toward her and spinning her around. "Do you see any wings growing out of this child?"

Uncle Arthur shook his head. "Of course not. But that signifies nothing."

"Nothing!" Cousin Prudence's voice rose sharply. "Well, I never!"

"Cousin," said the Earl, judging it was time to put period to this discussion. "Perhaps you and Mr. Amesley can continue this disagreement later. Right now I should like to have our guests shown to their rooms."

Cousin Prudence turned a little redder in the face, but she composed herself. "Of course, milord. This way please."

The men followed her and Phoebe, casting another of those strange looks at Aurelia, trailed after them.

"So," he said, crossing the room to the

divan and resuming his seat. "That went well enough."

"Yes, yes it did."

He raised an eyebrow. Was her voice trembling? "You did not add your arguments to mine. Do you not *want* to stay?"

"Oh, I . . . Actually, milord, I thought it best to remain silent. After taking the balloon as I did . . . Well, I didn't think having me argue the case would be much help."

Well, at least her understanding was good. He smiled. "Perhaps not. At any rate, I'm glad to have the pleasure of your company for a time longer."

Did he see a little flicker of warmth in her eyes? Or was she just being polite? It was most infernally annoying, being on tenterhooks like this. With any other female he would have known exactly where he stood. But with her . . .

He put on his warmest, most beguiling, smile, the one that had earned him the favors of many London ladies. "Tell me, Miss Amesley. Is there anything I can do to make your stay more pleasant?"

"Yes," she replied, looking him directly in the eyes. "I have a great desire to go horseback riding. How soon can you arrange it?"

Chapter

Seven

It was Tuesday afternoon before the Earl got around to arranging their ride. From her position in his arms, Aurelia looked over the animal that was supposed to advance The Plan.

"Are you sure you want to do this now?" the Earl inquired. "Your ankle . . ."

"Milord," she reminded him. "One rides sitting down."

"True."

"And I have such an inclination for a ride, a good rousing gallop."

The Earl sighed. She could feel it along the whole lean length of him.

"It's very kind of you to accommodate me like this," she continued. If he backed out now, The Plan would be ruined.

"Think nothing of it." He stood her carefully on her good foot. "Because of your injury, I shall help you mount in a different fashion."

He put a hand on either side of her waist

and lifted her quite easily onto the side-saddle. For a moment she was busy getting her leg properly hooked, gathering up the reins, and trying to recall all that Phoebe had told her about riding.

Finally, she was settled and looked down, only to discover that a horse brought one much higher off the ground than might have been expected. But that didn't bother her. After all, she had sailed through the heavens in a wicker basket.

She took a deep breath and adjusted the pert little shako hat that Phoebe had perched on her head. The green riding habit fit well enough. Now, if she only knew something about the actual act of riding.

The Earl swung up on his horse — a beautiful black creature, with glistening coat and tossing mane. "All set?"

She nodded. "Yes, let's go." She touched the horse with her heel and it went off obediently. Unfortunately, its jiggling gait threatened to bounce her right out of the saddle.

"Miss Amesley," the Earl called after her. "Please, do not trot just yet."

"Yes, yes," she called back over her shoulder. She pulled on the reins and miraculously the animal slowed. Maybe riding was not so difficult after all.

The Earl's horse moved up beside hers. "I'm most pleased with our work of the last two days," he said as they rode down the lane toward the meadow.

"Yes, Uncle Arthur is very happy at how the repairs are going."

The Earl smiled. He had such a pleasant smile. She wished she could be sitting some comfortable place with him, talking aeronautics. "But I still can't see why you want to build a *montgolfière*. Hot air is so old-fashioned."

He laughed. "Cousin Prudence doesn't think so. She's convinced we're going straight to perdition. The whole lot of us. For daring to invade the Good Lord's heavens."

Aurelia laughed, too. "Yes, I know. She is continually reciting Scriptures to me. But she means well."

For a moment they rode in silence. Then the Earl asked, "Do you think Harold means well?"

"Harold? I don't understand."

"Harold seems to be dangling after Phoebe. I am concerned about his intentions. After all, Phoebe is under my protection."

So he had noticed, too. She stalled for time. "What makes you think this?"

The Earl frowned. "For one thing, they are always together."

"Phoebe is much interested in aeronautics."

"She is now," he said dryly.

"Oh, no, milord. She had conceived this interest long before my family arrived. Before I arrived. She told me herself that she longs to go aloft. But her mama will never permit it."

The Earl's eyes gleamed with laughter. "I should say not." He gave her what should have been a stern look if his eyes had not spoiled it. "Let us hope that the story of your escapade doesn't give her ideas in that line."

"Ideas? Oh dear." Laughter bubbled from her and she clapped a hand to her mouth. And, of course, the animal she was riding chose that precise moment to leap forward and take off at a gallop.

Unfortunately, a good run was not nearly as pleasant as Phoebe had described it. To be bouncing up and down *and* sideways was most disconcerting. The horse paid no heed to her efforts to slow it down. It just ran, faster and faster.

"Aurelia!" the Earl called after her. "Miss Amesley, stop!"

"I cannot! Help!"

Sawing at the reins, she perceived that she was telling the awful truth. The horse had the bit between its teeth and was running for dear life.

Woodland and meadow passed in a whirlwind of confused images — a hassock of turf that almost unseated her, a low hanging branch she ducked to avoid, and, in the distance, a winding ribbon of stream.

The pounding of her horse's hooves almost drowned out her own labored breathing. She could not turn her head to see if he were coming. She could barely keep her seat.

The stream was getting closer — and wider. Surely it would stop the horse. But then, just as she expected the horse to slow, she felt it gather itself to jump.

"No-o-o-o-o!"

There was one long timeless moment when her body left the saddle. And then she was lying in the stream, making curious noises while she fought to pull air into her lungs.

The shako hat, which had fallen over her eyes, obscured her vision, but as her labored breathing slowed, she could hear the pounding of coming hooves.

She pushed herself to a sitting position and tugged off the offending hat. Her hair came down, spilling over her shoulders and dripping down her face. She pushed at it impatiently.

Cold water was running over her lap and she couldn't even get up to escape it. Her ankle was still too weak for tramping about the rocky bottoms of streams. She shifted. And this bottom was very rocky.

Ranfield pulled his mare to a halt. She appeared uninjured. Thank God! Sitting there in the middle of the stream, she made quite a sight. He felt the laughter rising in him, but he shoved it back down. A gentleman should not laugh at a lady in distress.

He dismounted. "Miss Amesley, are you hurt?"

"I think not." She threw a strand of wet hair out of her eyes. "But I cannot stand. I'm most dreadfully sorry, milord. But I fear I cannot get up without help."

She looked so contrite, sitting there. So innocent. And, strangely enough, sodden and rumpled, she looked beautiful. But where on earth had she learned to ride in that atrocious fashion?

He spared one regretful glance for his shining Wellingtons and then he stepped into the water. "I'll have you out in a minute." Wet as she was, he managed to lift her. But her habit was waterlogged and the stream bottom uneven. Halfway to shore his boot heel turned on a pebble. There was a brief moment of panic. And there he was — sitting in the stream with a sodden Miss Amesley in his lap.

A giggle escaped her. She buried her face in his waistcoat. Trying to contain it, no doubt. And he firmed his jaw.

But it was no use. Laughter overcame them both. And they sat there, in the middle of the stream, clutching each other, and laughed till they cried.

"I'm sorry," she said, finally, when she could speak again. "But the expression on your face . . ."

"No apologies are necessary." He was loathe to get up. He liked having her there in his lap, water and all. But he had to be sensible. And he certainly didn't want her to take a chill.

Gently he set her aside and heaved himself to his feet. His coat hung about him, a sodden mass. Water ran from his breeches in rivulets, and inside his boots it squelched between his toes.

He offered her his hand. "No apologies," he repeated. "But perhaps you had better walk out. Lean on me."

"Yes. Of course."

She bit her lip as though about to burst

into laughter again. He must look quite a sight. What a rare woman she was. Scatter-brained, surely the most horrible horse-woman in all of England. But also the most entertaining.

He smiled to himself. He knew no woman of the *ton* who would laugh in such a situation. Any of them would have cursed the horse and him — indiscriminately.

They made the bank safely, though not without a few giggles and coughs. She smiled up at him, those great dark eyes still gleaming with laughter.

"Thank you, milord. You're most kind." She looked down at his feet. "I'm dreadfully afraid I've ruined your boots and . . ." A shiver overtook her.

He wanted to wrap her in his arms to warm her. Instead he led her to the horses. "Let me help you mount. We must get you home and out of these wet things."

"Yes, milord. They are rather sodden."

She looked up at him again, her eyes pulling at him. And that delectable little mouth crying to be kissed. He leaned toward her, almost mesmerized. Just one little kiss . . .

Abruptly he straightened. One little kiss, indeed! Miss Amesley was a guest in his home. And she was no high-flier to flirt and play with. He had a feeling that Aurelia Amesley took things like kisses quite seriously. And, in her presence at least, so should he.

Aurelia shivered and swallowed a sigh. The habit was wet and heavy, dragging her down. But it was a mere hindrance. What frightened her — almost — was the look in his eyes. She longed to bury herself in their depths, to . . .

His hands spanned her waist again. And with one great heave he had her remounted. The heavy wet skirt made it difficult to move, and her memory of flying through the air was still quite strong. To say nothing of the crush of landing. But she refused to ask for help. Lady Incognita's heroines would brave anything to be with their men. Still, she had to admit as she gathered up the reins, the prospect of another runaway was decidedly unnerving.

Evidently, the Earl thought so, too. "I believe I shall lead this creature home. That could have been a bad spill."

He swung up into the saddle, still dripping water, and started out, with her horse trailing behind. She was dreadfully cold, but she would just watch the play of his shoulders as he moved and admire the way his dark hair curled over the back of his collar. That should warm her.

Unfortunately, by the time they'd reached the house, her body had refused to cooperate with her mind. She was chilled through and through, her teeth chattering with a will of their own.

The Earl lifted her down. His arms were warm and safe. She wanted to stay there, close to him. But the shivering continued:

"Please," she said. "Just help me walk. It will warm me."

"Of course."

Pratt, with his usual aplomb, had the door open before they reached it.

"Miss Amesley has had an accident," the Earl said. "Tell Mrs. Esterhill and Cousin Phoebe to bring hot water and blankets."

"Yes, milord."

By dint of much effort, and leaning heavily on the Earl, Aurelia reached her room. Because of her sodden condition, she dared not lie down, but stood, clutching the bedpost for support.

The Earl reached out, tucking a wet curl behind her ear. "Thank you," he said. "For a most interesting afternoon."

"Thank . . . me?" Of all things, why should she want to laugh again? But laugh she must.

So, when an anxious Phoebe, followed by her equally anxious mama, rushed into the room, it was to the sight of the two of them laughing uncontrollably.

Aurelia attempted to comport herself more sensibly. "My . . . my horse ran off," she managed. "But . . ."

The Earl did better. He suppressed his laughter and wiped his eyes. "But the animal jumped the stream. And Miss Amesley lost her seat. Better get her out of those wet things immediately." He looked down at himself. "And I shall do the same. Ladies, until dinner."

Before the door closed behind him, Phoebe was busy at the military frogs that closed the habit's jacket. "You are soaked."

"To the skin," Aurelia agreed. She knew Phoebe was bursting to have all the details, but how could she tell her anything with her mama right there?

Ten minutes later the Esterhills had Aurelia in bed in her nightdress with hot chocolate in her stomach, hot bricks to her feet, and enough covers to make it difficult to move.

"Now," said Cousin Prudence. "You just close your eyes. After a shock like that a body needs rest."

Phoebe sighed. "I'll just stay with her till she drops off."

Cousin Prudence gave her daughter a hard look. "You'll do no such thing. You're coming along with me."

"But . . ."

"Now."

Phoebe raised her eyes in a gesture of resignation and Aurelia mouthed the word later.

She meant to lie there and relive every moment of her not so propitious rescue. But all that warmth was doing its work, and before her thoughts got as far as the runaway, she was sound asleep.

When she woke, some time later, she was wearing a smile. In her dreams they'd been laughing together.

The door creaked. "I'm awake, Phoebe. Come in."

Phoebe needed no second invitation. She hurried to the bedside. "Aurelia, are you truly all right?"

"I'm fine."

Her face aglow with curiosity, Phoebe pulled up a chair. "Then tell me what happened."

"The horse ran away."

"Yes, I know that."

"And it threw me in the stream."

"I know that, too! Oh, Aurelia, don't

110

tease me so. I've been about to explode, waiting to hear what occurred."

"That's it. The horse threw me in. The Earl carried me out."

"And that's all?"

Phoebe looked so woebegone Aurelia could hardly keep from laughing. "Well, he picked me up and then he slipped. And fell. And we were both sitting there, in the water, laughing."

"Laughing?"

"Yes. I was in his lap, more or less, and we just got to laughing."

"Hmmm. In the water. Laughing." Phoebe reached in the desk for pen and ink. "Would you say this helped The Plan?"

"I don't know. He did rescue me. But I must have looked a fright. And he didn't say — or do — anything." There was that look she'd glimpsed in his eyes, that strange look she'd never seen before. But maybe she had imagined it. And, anyway, how could she be sure?

Phoebe waved the quill. "I'll put a question mark then." She consulted their list. "The next thing . . ."

Aurelia sighed. "Phoebe, please. Not today. It's a wonder the Earl was not all out of sorts. He ruined his clothes. And his boots. Oh, I hope he doesn't catch a chill."

"Of course he won't. Ranfield's constitution is par excellence." She waved the quill again, and an anxious expression wrinkled her brow. "Aurelia, would you explain to me? About balloons and air currents and all that? Young Mr. Amesley was telling me about them this afternoon. But . . ."

A blush suffused her cheeks. "But I was so conscious of the man himself that I could not follow what he was saying. Isn't that unusual?"

Aurelia smiled. "I think not," she said. "It sounds to me suspiciously like love."

Chapter

Eight

Wednesday afternoon found them all back at the shed hard at work on the balloon. Aurelia and Phoebe, seated in comfortable chairs, occupied themselves with stitching up the rents in the balloon, which billowed about them till they were almost lost from sight. Across the room the Earl and Harold worked with the wicker gondola.

Phoebe looked up from her stitching. "Tell me, Aurelia. When they put in the gas, why does it not escape through the holes our needles make?"

"That is a good question." Aurelia looked around.

Phoebe's eyes, too, turned to where the men, their shirt sleeves rolled up, were retouching the basket's battered paint.

Phoebe looked back. "You tell me, please. I do so want to understand. For Mr. Amesley's sake."

Aurelia smiled. Last night she and Phoebe had talked for a long time about

Harold. And this interest of hers in ballooning was a further sign . . .

"After we finish our mending, the men
will treat the balloon with something to
make the silk impenetrable. Sometimes they
use varnish. Sometimes something called
caoutchouc, which the French prefer."

Phoebe smiled. "I see. So then the gas or
the hot air cannot escape. Except when you
let it by pulling the valve rope."

"Yes," Aurelia replied. "That is it."

Phoebe wiggled in her chair, and the great
mass of silk made a sighing, almost human,
sound. "I do hope I get to go up," she said.

"But your mama . . ."

"I will handle Mama," Phoebe replied,
her chin jutting. "It is Mr. Amesley I'm worried about."

"Uncle Arthur?"

Phoebe giggled. "Of course not, you goose!"
A sudden frown wrinkled her forehead.
"Unless you think he would object to . . ."
She looked toward the men and colored.

"Oh, Phoebe, don't worry. Uncle Arthur
likes you." Aurelia smiled. "Besides, he
would not want to offend the Earl." Her
gaze went again to where Ranfield worked
beside Harold. Even in shirt sleeves the Earl
was a fine figure of a man.

He turned, almost as though he had felt

her gaze, and flashed her a smile. Before she even thought about it, she was smiling in return.

She was about to suggest to Phoebe that they leave their sewing for a moment to stretch their limbs and perhaps admire the new painting on the gondola.

But before she could do so, the door burst open and Cousin Prudence bustled in. She was followed by half a dozen liveried footmen whose expressions of bored detachment couldn't quite hide their curiosity.

"Put the table there," she ordered, pointing to a place near Aurelia. "And the chairs around it." And while the others watched in awe, Cousin Prudence set up for afternoon tea, complete with the silver service and Wedgwood china.

The Earl came forward, rolling down his shirt sleeves. "This was most kind of you, Cousin. But unnecessary. We could have returned to the house."

"Could have, perhaps." She eyed him sternly. "But wouldn't have." She marched over to Aurelia. "This young woman is still recovering from two life-threatening accidents."

Aurelia felt the blood rush to her cheeks. Cousin Prudence was too much given to the dramatic.

But the round little woman didn't even notice. She adjusted her cap and waved a pudgy hand. "The poor child has to have proper sustenance. And as for the rest of you — well, you might as well join her."

Before the Earl could finish his thanks, she had bustled out again. "Come, Harold," he said. "Let us join the ladies."

Soon the two of them were comfortably seated. Aurelia and Phoebe pushed the rustling silk aside and drew up their chairs.

"Miss Amesley," said the Earl. "Would you be so kind as to pour?"

"Of course, milord." Slowly and steadily she filled the delicate Wedgwood cups. Phoebe passed the plate of macaroons, and shortly they were all sipping and chattering as comfortably as in any drawing room.

"Perhaps my groom will return with the brazier today," the Earl remarked.

Aurelia shook her head. "I don't understand why you still favor hot air as a propellant. *Montgolfières* are so old-fashioned."

Ranfield smiled and sipped his tea. He did not particularly favor hot air. But he had no intention of giving Miss Amesley that particular information. He loved to hear her discourse on the advantages of hydrogen gas over hot air. Or, more to the point, he liked to watch her face as she waxed eloquent about some technical matter of aeronautics. And, if that matter were one she had covered before, so much the better. He could devote less time to listening and more time to looking.

He spared a glance to see how Harold was doing. Miss Amesley's cousin was gazing at Phoebe with calf's eyes. And Phoebe was returning the favor. Those two were obviously enamored of each other. So be it. His cousin could do far worse than Harold, who, though no aristocrat, was a gentleman in the truest sense.

He smiled to himself. Perhaps being around Phoebe would put Aurelia in a romantic mood. He had decided to call her Aurelia to himself. Though of course he could not address her that way. Yet.

He liked the way her name rolled on his tongue. He liked the way she looked, dark eyes sparkling, dainty hands waving. He liked everything about her.

Well, not everything, he amended hastily. She was by far the worst horsewoman he had ever encountered. And she had a rather disconcerting disposition toward life-endangering accidents. He hadn't needed to have Cousin Prudence point that out.

True, Miss Amesley's accidents had resulted in only minor injuries. But any fool could tell that a crashing balloon might well be fatal. And, as for falls from horseback, more than one Englishman had gone to meet his Maker after just such an event.

Two such incidents within a single week could give a man pause. Even if that man were taken with great dark eyes and a rosebud mouth. Of course, she was not actually a peabrain. For example, she knew much more about aeronautics than he did. And she had retained much of her education. After all, hadn't she remembered Dr. Johnson's words about the novel?

"Hey, Ranny?"

"Yes, Harold."

"Leave off woolgathering and tell us about the balloon you've ordered."

"Yes. Well, I told them to rush. I want to go up this summer. Let's see. It's 30 feet in diameter."

He glanced at Aurelia. Her face was wreathed in a smile. Would he ever mean as much to her as air flight did? He pushed the thought aside and turned back to her cousin. "Perhaps when your balloon is repaired, you'll give me some lessons in flying."

"Be glad to," said Harold. But his glance at Phoebe told plainly whom he preferred as companion. He ran a hand through his hair.

"Say, Reely can do it. She can take you up and show you the works."

"But Uncle Arthur won't let me go up. You know that, Harold."

Harold grinned. "For once you're wrong. Papa told me just today — before he left for the supplies. He's not going to stand in your way. He's going to teach you all he knows."

Watching her, Ranfield saw her face register shock. And elation. "But his promise . . ."

Harold shrugged. "It's broken already. Besides, he says he never felt right about it. Says it ain't fair to bring up a child in the way you want it to go and then say it can't. Says he'd never have promised if your papa hadn't caught him by surprise, and him dying like that."

Ranfield frowned. He wasn't sure he liked this change of sentiment. It was one thing to listen to her talk. Quite another to have her sailing off.

And in a flimsy wicker basket. He cast a glance at the gondola, which seemed to have grown decidedly smaller and more fragile. He could summon many arguments against females in air flight.

But one look at her face told him that all his words would be useless. Worse than useless, actually, for they would turn her against him — and without at all changing her mind about flight.

He swallowed his words of caution and extended a hand. "Congratulations, Miss Amesley. I know this means a great deal to you."

Still stunned by the enormity of Harold's news, Aurelia automatically put out her hand. The Earl's fingers were warm; the grip, firm and strong.

How kind of him to congratulate her — and to understand. Most men would have been quite adamant against female aeronauts.

She nibbled on a macaroon and watched Phoebe turn to Harold. "Have there been many female aeronauts?" Phoebe asked.

Harold's freckles stood out on his fair skin. His smile threatened to split his face. "A few, Miss Esterhill. The first in England was a Mrs. Sage. She went up . . ." He looked to Aurelia.

"In June of '85."

"That's right." Harold grinned. "My head's full of air currents and such. No room in there for dates. You tell it, Reely."

"There's not much to tell. She went up at St. George's Field, the amusement garden at Newington Butts. And she came down safely."

"And of course there is Madame Blanchard," Harold continued. "She has been going aloft for many, many years. And quite safely."

"Nevertheless," remarked the Earl, "there have been accidents. The *charlières* can explode. Hydrogen gas is quite flammable."

Aurelia felt a pang of fear. *He* could not mean to forbid her air flight. "*Montgolfières* can also catch fire," she said, keeping her voice calm. "But not if precautions are taken."

"Precautions," the Earl repeated.

"Yes, aeronauts are trained to be careful."

"But even care may not prevent all mischances."

She could think of no more to say. Why must he have such an incisive mind, cutting right to the quick of things?

The four of them lapsed into silence, sipping their tea.

Aurelia had just returned her cup to her saucer when the door opened again. "Miserable female," Uncle Arthur was murmuring. "Oh woman, thy tongue is venom."

Harold got to his feet. "Papa, what is it? What's wrong?"

"It's that woman." Uncle Arthur ran a hand across his bald pate. "Begging your pardon, milord, seeing as she's your relative and all. But she's monstrous persistent. Wears a man down with her Scriptures." He grinned ruefully. "Seems like she's always got one at hand. Or two or three."

The Earl stood up. "Well," he said, clapping Uncle Arthur on the back. "It looks like you'll have to take up Scripture reading yourself."

Uncle Arthur's face was a study in perplexity. "I, your lordship?"

"Of course. So you can find material to refute her."

Her uncle considered this, then shook his head. "That woman can't be refuted. That woman is . . . is granite."

The Earl laughed. "But the Scriptures can move her. If you find the right passage." He raised an eyebrow. "To the best of my knowledge she hasn't yet found any that expressly forbid air flight. So perhaps you can find one that seems to praise it."

Uncle Arthur shook his head again. "I shall certainly try. But come, let's get to work on those lashings."

The men moved off, and Phoebe and Aurelia returned to their stitching. But Phoebe looked worried. "Is it really so dangerous?" she asked, finally.

Aurelia considered this. "It's as Harold said. People die in many fashions. But we are careful, and so it is not that dangerous."

She smiled. "Do not frown so. It will wrinkle your fair skin."

Phoebe grimaced. "Please, do not mention wrinkles to Mama. She will be after me with her foul-smelling lotions. And some Scriptures, too."

Aurelia laughed. "Then you must smile."

Phoebe complied. "Very well, I shall try. But listen, should you not be working on The Plan?"

Aurelia nodded. "I am. But Phoebe, it is not easy to fall into a man's arms when he is already carrying you about."

Chapter
Nine

The next afternoon the Earl loaded them all into a phaeton and drove them to the meadow. Aurelia, watching him from her place beside Uncle Arthur, wondered again how any man could look so elegantly turned out. There was never a wrinkle in the Earl's coat of blue superfine. His inexpressibles were always spotless. And his boots looked like dust would never dare to deface them.

"Is this not an ideal spot for ascensions?" he asked from the driver's seat as he stopped the horses.

"Yes," said all the Amesleys together, looking out across the meadow. "Ideal."

"Ideal," echoed Phoebe, her eyes on Harold.

"Perhaps you'd care to walk about," the Earl suggested. "Examine the terrain."

Harold hurried to help Phoebe out. "Capital idea," he declared.

"Yes," Uncle Arthur agreed. "I'll just take a stroll. Get the feel of the place."

As the others meandered off, Aurelia regarded the meadow. Her ankle was much better. She was able to move about the house without help, only favoring it a little, and being careful because the slippers borrowed from Phoebe were a trifle loose on her. But this turf looked very uneven. If she turned her ankle again! Momentarily she lost herself in visions of being carried about in the Earl's arms once more. But the vision was only momentary.

"So," said the Earl, turning toward her with that smile that made her heart jump. "What should you like to do?"

His question made her heart jump even faster. But, since she could never say aloud what she was thinking, she contented herself with a smile. "I should like to climb that tree — the spreading oak there on the edge of the meadow."

He looked perplexed, perhaps stunned was a better word. "You want to climb a tree?"

"Yes, milord. To look out over the entire scene. And to test the air currents."

His eyes were glowing at her. For a second, in memory, she was sitting in the stream with his arms around her, while they laughed and laughed. If only he would put his arms around her now. He would not, of course, because he was a gentleman.

She sighed and, hearing herself, sighed again. Lady Incognita's heroines sighed often. It was almost second nature to them. And she was beginning to see why.

Phoebe and Harold were already walking across the meadow — very close to each other. It was a pleasant sight. But shy as Harold was, Aurelia could not imagine he would speak soon. Phoebe was apt to get impatient.

Uncle Arthur had gone in the opposite direction, muttering about various wind currents and prodding the turf with the toe of his half-boot.

The Earl shook himself out of his bemused state. "Do you climb trees often?" he inquired.

Aurelia shook her head. "Not any more. When I was young, I did. It was quite entertaining."

She liked his smile. It made him even handsomer. If that were possible. "Didn't you climb . . . ?"

"Oh, yes," he replied. "But I wasn't hampered by a gown." He studied hers, then raised an eyebrow. "Frankly, I don't think you can do it in that rig."

She saw by his eyes that he was teasing her, but she frowned. "Then I shall have to prove you wrong."

"Aurel— Miss Amesley. Please. You have already had . . ."

She turned away and began to descend from the phaeton. Her head was a little light, and her breathing too rapid. But that was from hearing her Christian name on his lips. Or almost hearing it. Why must stupid convention insist on formality when she longed to hear him call her Aurelia?

She reached the turf while he was still tying the horses. Without waiting, she began to make her way toward the huge oak.

"Miss Amesley, stop. Let me help you."

He offered her his arm. She took it, remembering that first day at the Minerva when he had escorted her inside. There was no need to recall her sensations of that day. They were quite the same now. Only more intense. More exhilarating.

She did not really want to climb a tree. She wanted . . . She pushed the thought aside. To get what she wanted, she must follow The Plan. And The Plan said to climb a tree.

They reached the oak and stood looking up. It was a fine tree for climbing, with good strong branches nicely spaced, its foliage not too closely packed.

The Earl frowned. "Really, Miss Amesley.

This hardly seems necessary."

She wished it were not. She wished he would just declare himself. But since he did not, The Plan must be heeded.

"I wish to show you that females are quite as capable as males at climbing trees. And at other things — like aeronautics."

"There's no need . . . ," he began.

But she cut him off. "Your hands, please."

Obediently he cupped his hands so she could step into them.

"Now," she said, "when I get up, you will turn your back."

He looked up at her. "Turn . . . ?"

"Yes, of course. As you pointed out, this rig isn't exactly suitable for climbing trees."

He sighed, but he nodded. "Just do not fall. Dr. Monkton is very busy this week."

His mouth was laughing, but his eyes were worried. Did that mean . . . ?

She stepped into his hands, and seconds later she was standing on the first big branch. He kept his gaze away from her, but even so it was difficult climbing about with a long dress dragging at her. It was not her old bombazine either, but one of Phoebe's pretty gowns, a light concoction of yellow material, the color of sunshine. Its stylish long sleeves made reaching rather difficult.

And if the gown should split across the shoulders . . . But she had to go up before she could come down. And The Plan must be heeded.

So she made her way higher and higher, planting each kid slipper carefully before she moved the other. She'd climbed many a tree as a girl, and the old skills came back. Without the hindrance of the gown, it would have been easy.

Finally, she could go no farther. Leaning against the great trunk, she paused to catch her breath and take a long look at the sunny meadow. It was quite a pretty sight, framed by the green young leaves. Finally, she called down, "You may look now."

Ranfield was already looking. For some moments she'd been too occupied to notice him. Twice, when she came to a particularly difficult place, he'd opened his mouth to order her down. And twice he'd closed it again without saying anything. Aurelia Amesley was not the sort of woman one ordered about.

He caught his breath. She looked so small up there. Enchanted. Like an ancient wood nymph. Or a spring sunbeam among the green leaves. "So," he inquired. "How does one test the wind?"

She smiled down at him. "You wet your

finger and hold it up." She demonstrated.

He swallowed a sharp exclamation. Surely she could have done that on the ground. But there was no point in remonstrating with her. Better to take himself to task. How could he possibly fix his interest on such a woman? She would make his life one imbroglio after another.

"Turn again," she called. "I'm coming back down."

"But the last branch . . . You will need me."

"I shall tell you when I reach it."

He swallowed an oath and turned to look out across the meadow. But he saw nothing. All his senses were focused on the tree behind him and that peaheaded female descending from it. If she fell . . .

Finally, after what seemed hours, she called, "You may turn again."

And there she was, standing on the lowest branch, lovely as an angel and exasperating as an imp of Satan. He moved closer. He would breathe easier once her feet were on solid ground. "Let me help you."

Aurelia's heart commenced beating faster. He was so "heroish," standing there with that worried look on his face. Now all she had to do was slide nicely down into his arms and look up into his face. And he would kiss her. At least, according to The Plan, that's what he was supposed to do.

He raised his arms, and she stepped away from the trunk. One minute she was balancing fine, and the next, her slipper slid on the bark. "Oh, no!"

She flew out of the tree, her slippers catching him full in the waistcoat. She had time only to see his look of utter astonishment before he cried out and fell backward. Seconds later he was supine on the grass, and she was sitting on his chest.

"Oh dear!" She scrambled off to kneel beside him. "Milord? Ranfield?"

His eyes were closed, and he seemed so pale. She stretched out a tentative hand and felt his cheek. A terrible tenderness washed over her and tears sprang to her eyes. If only she had the right to gather him in her arms. Oh, what should she do?

And then his eyes opened. They were still a little glazed, but gradually they focused on her. "Are . . . you hurt?" he asked.

"Oh no! You . . . you stopped my fall quite nicely."

Slowly he raised himself to a sitting position and put a hand to his head. "I'm glad to be of service," he said, with a spark of his old humor.

"Glad . . ." She could not laugh, not until

she knew. "Are *you* hurt?"

He felt his limbs, then slowly shook his head. "I think not. Just a little winded."

He frowned. "What happened this time?"

"It was the slipper. They're Phoebe's, you know. And a trifle large. I just slipped. On the bark. Oh, I am so sorry."

Ranfield considered this while he caught his breath. She did, indeed, look sorry. And he found it was worth having the wind knocked out of him to see her looking at him like that, to see concern on her pretty face. But this kind of thing could not go on. "Really, Miss Amesley, misfortune seems to dog your footsteps. Has it always been so?"

She colored, the blood tinting her cheeks a healthy — and delectable — pink.

"Oh no, milord. My accident with the balloon was the very first. I have climbed many trees and never slipped before."

"And the runaway horse?"

More color rose to her cheeks. What did they mean, those blushes?

She looked away from him. "I . . . I had never had any riding accidents either, before the other day."

There was something more here, something he couldn't understand, that accounted for her peculiar behavior. But until he knew what it was, he couldn't seriously consider asking her . . . He shouldn't be considering it at all.

He pushed himself to his feet and dusted off his clothes. She continued to kneel there, the yellow gown spread around her, her great dark eyes so contrite. She was so beautiful. For one glorious second he let himself imagine taking her in his arms and kissing away that frown. Then he shook himself. Not yet. Perhaps not ever. He offered her his hand. "Come, let's find the others."

It was some hours later, their excursion over, before the two young women found themselves alone. As they approached her room, Aurelia waited for the rush of questions, but Phoebe was strangely quiet. She followed Aurelia into the room and sank into a chair, staring vacantly into space.

Aurelia turned to look at her. "Phoebe, dear, are you ill?"

"What?" Phoebe smiled. "Oh, no. I am just thinking."

Aurelia sat down on the chaise. "About Harold, no doubt."

Phoebe blushed prettily. "Yes. About him." She sighed and went back to staring vacantly.

Aurelia gnawed her lower lip. Phoebe was

badly afflicted. "Is there anything I can do to help?"

Phoebe shook her head. "Oh, no. It's just . . . Oh, Aurelia, I feel so peculiar. Especially when he's about. I . . . ." She paused and raised a hand to her mouth. "Oh, my dear! I clean forgot. The Plan. How did it go?"

Aurelia frowned. "Not as we intended."

"What happened?"

"He let me climb the tree."

"Yes?"

"And I managed that fine. Got way up. But when it was time to come down, I slipped." She covered her face with her hands. "Oh, it was the most horrible thing. I was all ready to slide gracefully into his arms, my face upturned. And . . . and . . ."

"Oh, do tell me!"

"And I slid off and hit him full in the waistcoat. It knocked him out. And then I landed on top of him."

"Oh, dear!" Phoebe looked uncertain whether to laugh or cry.

"I got right off, of course. And he came to. I knelt right there, like Corrinne did. But when he helped me up, nothing happened."

"Nothing happened." Phoebe sighed. "It was the same with Harold and me."

"You fell on Harold?"

"Oh, no. I mean, nothing happened."

"But you looked quite happy together."

"Perhaps so. But he did not kiss me."

"Phoebe! It is only Thursday. Harold has not even known you for a whole week."

"And how long did the dark stranger know Corrinne before he swept her up in his arms and declared that his heart was forever hers?"

"Not long," Aurelia said. "But Phoebe, Harold is not the dark stranger. Harold is very shy." She took a turn around the room. "Phoebe, I'm not sure The Plan is going to work. Perhaps we have made a mistake thinking this way."

"Nonsense!" For a moment Phoebe became her usual brisk self. "It has to work. You must marry Ranfield."

"But I keep having these accidents."

Phoebe frowned. "Was he irate? Did he fly up in the boughs over what happened?"

"Oh no. He was very polite and concerned for my welfare."

"Did he look like he wanted to" — Phoebe lowered her voice and glanced at the closed door — "kiss you?"

"When he helped me up . . . I thought . . . There was warmth in his eyes. But he didn't."

Phoebe considered her plaited fingers and

then she raised her head and smiled. "That's it," she announced. "It's too soon for both of them. We shall have to be patient."

Chapter

Ten

In the days that followed, both young women found their patience worn thin. Every day was spent working on the balloons. Great progress was made with aeronautics, but romance remained at a standstill.

Two weeks of intensified labor had the Amesley balloon repaired and ready to fly. One afternoon, Aurelia and Phoebe stood watching while Uncle Arthur supervised the unloading of the barrels of iron filings and the jugs of chemicals that would be poured into them to form the hydrogen gas.

The Earl and Harold came to stand beside them. "In a day or two," Harold said to the Earl, "your balloon will be going up. We've got the brazier. And everything looks good."

"How I should love to fly," Phoebe breathed, her eyes on Harold.

"I should like to take you," he replied. "But your mama . . ."

"Let us leave the first flights to more seasoned aeronauts," the Earl suggested to Phoebe. "Miss Amesley and Harold should go up first. You and I will have our turn later."

Phoebe stared at him. "Really, Ranfield? You mean I shall actually get to go up? You promise? Oh, how marvelous."

Aurelia smiled, pleased with her friend's happiness, pleased, too, with her own. At least something had gone right. Uncle Arthur had confirmed that he no longer felt constrained by his promise to her father. He asked only one thing of her — that she not go up alone. And, of course, she had agreed.

The prospect of being aloft again made her feel quite light-headed. And if part of that light-headedness came from the knowledge that she and the Earl might share a flight . . . Well, it was a breathtaking thought.

The Earl cast a satisfied glance around him. "We have worked hard," he said. "So tomorrow we will take a day off. We'll have a little excursion to Pirates' Cave."

His eyes met Aurelia's. "I'll have Cook pack a luncheon. We'll eat by the sea."

She smiled at him. He was remembering his promise. "That sounds most entertaining."

Harold, his eyes on Phoebe, nodded.

"Yes. We all need a rest."

The Earl looked at her uncle. "And you, sir. Will you join us?"

Uncle Arthur smiled. "The sea holds no delight for me. I believe I'll spend the day searching the Scriptures. Perhaps I can find something to silence that woman."

Aurelia laughed with the others. But it was not like Uncle Arthur to care what people said. As he often remarked, those who espoused new and startling ideas should always expect those ideas to be disregarded and themselves to be ridiculed. So why, then, was he letting Cousin Prudence have such an effect on him?

Aurelia cast a quick glance at her cousin, gazing unabashedly at Phoebe. That must be it. Uncle Arthur was aware of Harold's interest in Phoebe. And he wanted to bring her mama around.

Aurelia sighed. Cousin Prudence was no easy nut to crack. As adamant as she was against any kind of air flight, it was difficult to see how her mind could ever be persuaded otherwise.

They started out after breakfast the next morning. This time the Earl left the driving to a groom and took his place on the seat beside Aurelia. He flashed her a smile that made her knees go to trembling. She smiled in return and pulled the India shawl closer, thinking to herself that the Earl had been very generous to his cousin. Phoebe's wardrobe contained many lovely gowns. At the moment, Aurelia was wearing a dove gray walking dress. And Phoebe was attired in one of pale green. Between the two of them they had not yet exhausted Phoebe's supply of gowns and gloves, shawls and bonnets.

Aurelia tugged at the bonnet she was wearing, a straw affair trimmed with yellow roses and threaded through with a lemon yellow scarf that tied, fetchingly so Phoebe said, under her chin.

Though at first she'd been more comfortable in her old bombazine, now she was beginning to feel relaxed in these pretty things. And perhaps, as Phoebe kept insisting, pretty gowns would advance The Plan.

The phaeton halted at the top of the cliffs. Aurelia drew in a deep breath. The fresh damp air carried the tang of salt. Before them the great expanse of water stretched as far as the eye could see. Sunlight gleamed on the crests of the waves and danced in the shimmering foam.

"Oh, it is lovely!"

The Earl smiled. "We shall have to go on foot from here." He stepped down and offered her his gloved hand.

When she put her fingers in his, it happened again. That pleasant, breathless sensation stole over her.

He led her toward the cliffs. "The Pirates' Cave is down there," he said. "Do you think you can manage the path?"

It was rather a steep path, but Phoebe, who had been there before, had suggested walking boots. "Oh, yes," Aurelia said. "My ankle is quite healed and I am eager to see where the pirates come."

Harold's face took on a peculiar expression. "I take it there's no likelihood of pirates using the caves now." He sent a cherishing glance at Phoebe. "After all, we got to think of the ladies."

The Earl smiled. "Put your heart at ease, Harold. These were pirates of long ago. It's possible smugglers may use the caves. But certainly not in daylight."

He offered Aurelia his hand. "May I help you down the path?"

For a second she hesitated. She wanted to take his hand, and the reason to do so was legitimate. It was just that he made her so breathless. And somehow, when she was around him . . . These accidents kept . . .

She put her hand in his. This time she would do something without mishap. The

Earl had been seeing her through far too many scrapes.

Halfway down, her boot twisted on a pebble, and she was brought up hard against him. For a terrible second she had visions of them both tumbling, head over heels, down the rocky path. But his grip was firm, and he steadied her until she recovered her balance.

She would have regained it far quicker if her hand had not chanced to land against his brocaded waistcoat where it felt, quite distinctly, the beating of his heart. And then, when she naturally gazed up into his eyes, she caught a look that set her own heart leaping about in the most frightful fashion.

It took her several moments, but slowly she pulled her eyes away and resumed her descent. They reached the bottom with no further ado, there to find Phoebe and Harold waiting. Those two, gazing at each other, seemed to emit a glow that rivaled the sunshine on the waves.

The sand was soft under her boots, making it difficult to walk. But the Earl tucked her arm through his. "This way," he said, rounding a huge wet boulder.

The caves were dark — damp and musty. "When the tide comes in, the water covers the entrance."

Phoebe shivered dramatically and drew closer to Harold. Aurelia noticed he did not move away.

"Tell them the story, Ranfield," Phoebe urged. "It's so deliciously dreadful."

The Earl shook his head, and his laughter rumbled out, echoing in the caves. "Very well, my bloodthirsty cousin."

His gaze returned to Aurelia. "Pirates used to rendezvous here." He pointed into the gloom. "They stored their booty high up in the caves, where the water couldn't reach."

Aurelia looked at the narrow paths along the ledges. "Can we go back there?"

"If we are careful." He took her hand and drew her after him, up the ledge and then along it. Phoebe and Harold followed.

The farther they got from the patch of sunlight that marked the entrance, the less Aurelia liked it. But she didn't intend to let the Earl know. Lady Incognita's heroines braved untold dangers to be with their men. She covered a smile. Perhaps that accounted for their so often having to be rescued.

Finally, they reached the farther recesses of the cave. It was not a particularly pleasant spot — dark and dank and with a chill that cut into the bones.

"The story," Phoebe repeated, her eyes glowing in the gloom. "Finish the story."

"Patience, my dear. Give me a moment." Ranfield frowned. Strange how Phoebe liked such frightening things. He'd read some of those romances of terror she adored — and they could be quite disturbing.

But he couldn't imagine Aurelia — he savored the sound of her name even in his mind — being afraid of anything. After all, it took a great deal of nerve to go aloft in a wicker basket. And all alone like that.

"Ranfield! The story."

He discovered them all staring at him. "Yes, yes. Of course. The story goes that one of the pirates was wounded. His mates wouldn't take him to a doctor — afraid of getting caught, I suppose. So they left him here to die."

"Proper conduct for pirates, no doubt," said Harold, with an obvious attempt at humor.

"Quite so," Ranfield agreed.

Phoebe flashed him a glance. "The story. Finish the story."

"Well, the story goes that the next time they were leaving here, a hand came up out of the water and overturned the boat." He paused to let Phoebe enjoy the horror of it. "All but one of the crew managed to reach a ledge and crawl out. But that one vanished."

"Vanished," Phoebe whispered. "The dead man took his revenge."

Harold frowned. His voice boomed in the small space. "Really, my dear. Dead men do not overturn boats."

Phoebe frowned. She was not to be cheated of her terror. "This one did. There's more to the story, too. Every time the pirates came back, their boat was overturned and another crew member vanished." She shivered. "After they lost four, no one would come here any more."

The two young women exchanged glances and smiled. Ranfield frowned. What were those two up to now? "Come," he said. "It's time for our lunch."

"It was a delightful afternoon." Aurelia looked to Phoebe as they entered the room and cast their bonnets upon a lyre-back chair.

Phoebe nodded. "Yes, but I am not a patient person. Mr. Amesley has now known me above two weeks. When will he ask the question?"

"Phoebe, dear." Aurelia tried for a patience she herself didn't feel. "We must give them time. Picking a life partner is not to be done hastily."

Phoebe sighed. "I know. It's just that

145

when he looks at me in that way . . . Oh, I do so long to be Mrs. Harold Amesley!"

"And you shall. I'm certain of it." Aurelia could not forebear a little smile. Phoebe's sighs were overly dramatic. "I know Harold. He will come to the sticking point. But he is very shy. Just give him time."

"Time!" Phoebe cried. "Time is passing me by!"

Aurelia could not help it. She broke into laughter.

"My best friend," Phoebe intoned. "And she laughs at my heartbreak."

Aurelia swallowed a giggle. "Harold is as steady as they come," she said. "He would never break your heart."

"I know." Phoebe smiled wistfully. "But I do wish he would hurry." She took a turn around the room. "If only we had some sort of villain from whom he could rescue me. That did the trick for Corrinne."

"Phoebe, there are no villains here. No pirates. No smugglers."

Phoebe's eyes danced. "But if there were . . ."

"I'm sure Harold would do his best. But you would not really want to put him in danger."

"No, no. Of course not." She giggled. "Perhaps . . ."

By now Aurelia knew that look. "Phoebe Esterhill, what are you thinking?"

"Nothing, nothing. Only perhaps I shall go for a horseback ride."

Aurelia smiled. "That will not serve, my dear. Harold does not ride."

Phoebe frowned. "Well, then, we'll have to think of something else."

"We?"

"We," Phoebe replied firmly. "After all, we're in this thing together."

Chapter

Eleven

The next morning the four of them stood in a circle surveying the mounding pile of silk that had become Ranfield's balloon and the wicker basket that would hang beneath it.

Aurelia had to admit that it was a competent rig — for hot air. And, of course, hot air was much more economical, especially for short hops such as they had planned.

Phoebe looked at Harold and widened her eyes in alarm. "It's such a small basket," she cried. "How can one ascend into the heavens in . . . in a basket?"

It was much too exaggerated an alarm. Aurelia wished she had thought to warn Phoebe against carrying her fear so far. But Harold was too enamored even to notice. And the Earl, who might have been expected to be more aware, only looked a little thoughtful.

Stepping closer, Harold took Phoebe's hand in his and patted it comfortingly. "There's nothing to be frightened of, my dear," he said. "The gondola is quite sturdy."

Aurelia swallowed her laughter. How could Harold be so gullible? Why didn't he wonder when Phoebe, who had been dying to go aloft, suddenly became so fearful?

But Harold seemed completely taken in. He turned to the Earl in what was obviously an attempt to divert Phoebe's thoughts to more pleasant matters. "How do you plan to decorate your rig, Ranny? As I recall reading, Blanchard's balloon was of brilliant blue and gold. And his gondola was spangled blue." He smiled. "It must have been a marvelous sight."

The Earl laughed. She loved the sound of his laughter. Perhaps because it reminded her of those magical moments in the middle of the stream.

"No doubt," he said. "But I am not a showman. My interests are purely scientific. So I'm afraid my balloon will be plain silk, and the gondola will remain plain wicker."

Harold shook his head. "Too bad. Monsieur Blanchard was a man of science, too. But he understood the value of spectacle. Papa always says . . ."

Uncle Arthur came from around the corner. "What does Papa always say?"

"That if you want people to support scientific advancements like air flight, you've got to give them a show."

Uncle Arthur beamed. "Quite right, my boy. Quite right." He turned to Aurelia. "So, my dear, are you ready to try out the Earl's balloon?"

"Oh yes. Of course." These last days her thoughts had been so entangled with the Earl that she had almost forgotten the glory of flight. Indeed, sometimes getting The Plan to work seemed even more important than going aloft. But that could not really be so. Air flight was her life. She was glad to be going up, even if it was in a *montgolfière* and not their hydrogen balloon.

Uncle Arthur turned to the Earl. "Everything looks good. If it's all right with you, we'll have it carted out to the meadow and go up after lunch. It won't take long to get the brazier going. It's not like producing hydrogen gas, you know. That takes long hours."

Ranfield nodded and kept his face calm. He'd been anticipating this event for some days now — and not with joy. The thought of Aurelia ascending skyward, without him beside her, gave him a decidedly uneasy feeling. He did not voice it, however, but contented himself with asking, in as steady a voice as he could muster, "Harold's going up, too?"

"Oh yes," her uncle said. "Aurelia has promised not to go up alone."

The Earl nodded. He supposed he would have to be satisfied with that. At least Harold was a sound man, sensible, not given to taking chances.

And then Harold said, "I don't have my aeronautical outfit along."

"Outfit?" Phoebe inquired. The chit was hanging on Harold's every word. It must be most gratifying. Now if Aurelia would . . .

"Yes," Harold replied. "When I go up, I usually wear a scarlet coat, decorated with gold braid. And a red feather in my beaver."

The Earl suppressed a shudder. The great Beau Brummel's dictum of simplicity had obviously left no mark on Harold. "Isn't that a trifle . . . gaudy?"

Harold shrugged. "Men of science are above such considerations. The great Blanchard himself wore a tight blue suit." He grinned. "To match his balloon, no doubt. And a cocked hat set off with white feathers. I imagine he was quite a sight."

"Quite."

Shortly after lunch they arrived at the

151

meadow. Aurelia's heart lifted as she caught sight of the balloon, tugging gently at its tethers. She was going to fly again! It hardly seemed possible that Uncle Arthur had reversed his decision. But it was true.

As the Earl busied himself tying the horses, she turned to her uncle. "When can we take the Earl up?"

Uncle Arthur rubbed his bald pate. "Better let Harold show him the ropes."

Her heart dropped faster than a bag of sand ballast. "But Uncle, you said . . ." Something seemed to have lodged in her throat. It was so difficult to talk.

Uncle Arthur frowned. "I know, I said you could go up. But not alone."

"But she won't be alone."

She had not seen the Earl come round the carriage, but there he stood. "I'm sure Miss Amesley knows everything there is to know about ballooning."

She held her breath. She wanted this so much . . . to have him beside her up there.

"Really, sir," he went on. "Miss Amesley strikes me as a most sensible young woman. And you have surely taught her everything she needs to know."

He smiled. How, Aurelia wondered, could the same smile have such different effects on people? Surely it didn't make Uncle

Arthur go weak in the knees or start *his* heart to palpitating.

That thought made her swallow a smile. She much doubted if anything except ballooning had ever made Uncle Arthur's heart beat harder.

But, however different the smile's effect, it did its work. Uncle Arthur rubbed his pate once more and said, "Well, I suppose that would be all right. Next time. After all, Aurelia's as smart as they come."

This unexpected compliment nearly numbed her. Imagine Uncle Arthur saying a thing like that!

The Earl extended his hand to her. His eyes were sparkling, almost as though he knew how pleased she was feeling. "May I help you down?"

Minutes later, she and Harold were standing in the gondola.

"A short flight now," Uncle Arthur said. "There's plenty of straw for the brazier, but I don't want you to go flying away."

He directed a look at Aurelia that made her want to lower her head. Instead she nodded. "I understand, Uncle. We shall be very careful."

"Good. Then cast off."

The lines fell away. Aurelia, sending a last look at the Earl, saw him frowning. Now what was wrong? She sighed. Any number of things could be bothering him. She could only hope that this one didn't have to do with her — or with ballooning.

In truth, Ranfield was giving himself a good scold. The very idea of an Earl becoming enamored of a female aeronaut! He must have bats in his attic.

His father would be whirling in his grave. And Mama . . . Ranfield's frown turned into a smile. Mama would have asked about his feelings. Mama always got down to the important things.

"Oh," said Phoebe, from her place beside him. "Flying looks so wonderful. And Aurelia . . ."

He turned to his cousin. "You like Aurelia, don't you, Phoebe?"

She stared at him. "Like her? Oh, I do indeed. I wish, I wish she were my sister. I wish the Amesleys need never ever leave here."

"I see." He was a little taken back by her vehemence. But then, she obviously had a *tendre* for Harold.

She was gazing at him so intently, almost as though she expected him to make a comment. Or to reassure her that the Amesleys would stay on. But he curbed his tongue. As close as Phoebe was to Aurelia, he dared not say what he was thinking.

So he turned his gaze skyward again — and immediately wished he hadn't. The balloon was going higher and higher. He watched it become smaller and smaller. And found himself gritting his teeth.

Why did he have to feel as he did about Aurelia Amesley? Why, in all his years on the town, hadn't he been taken by a sweet young thing, suitably blooded and educated, reared to be an Earl's wife?

Because, said a mocking voice that sounded remarkably like his own, such a woman was dreadfully boring. Often empty-headed and, oftener still, entirely lacking in any redeeming values, except perhaps, innocence.

And if innocence were to be a criterion, Aurelia Amesley would score as high as any. The truth was that Aurelia scored high in all the qualities he found preferable in a wife. Except for her exasperating proclivity for accidents, she comported herself well. And she could learn what was necessary to get along in the city.

He smiled to himself. He suspected that with Aurelia as his spouse, life in the country would take on new enticements. And, his eyes still on the balloon, he fell to considering these.

He was still considering, when the balloon came floating back down and the men ran to grab the tether ropes. Harold leaped out, grinning widely. He pumped Ranfield's hand. "It's great, Ranny. Wait'll you get up there."

Aurelia's cheeks were pink, and her eyes shone with a glory Ranfield wished he'd been the cause of.

"Oh," she breathed, leaning over the gondola toward him. "It's the most glorious thing. There are no words to describe it."

He felt a distinct pang of jealousy. He'd seen women with that glow before. But never over a balloon.

She turned to her uncle. "Please, sir. The air currents are quite stable. Can't the Earl go up a little?"

Her uncle hesitated and Ranfield stepped forward. If she wanted him to go up in a balloon, he would go up in a balloon. "Just a short ride, Mr. Amesley. Surely that can come to no harm. I promise you, we won't go far."

Amesley's hand went to his bald pate, and he glanced at the sky. "I suppose it will be all right. Just be careful."

Ranfield nodded and swung himself into the basket. It moved slightly under his feet — a curious sensation.

"Ready?" asked Harold from his post by the rope.

"Ready," Aurelia replied and then looked to Ranfield. "That is . . ."

"You're the captain of this expedition," he replied. "Just tell me what to do."

She took him at his word. No fluttering lashes, no simpering looks. Just orders.

"A little straw on the brazier. Just a little. That's it. All right, Harold. We're ready."

Slowly the balloon rose. Ranfield sucked in his breath. He had forgotten the wonder of it. Of seeing everything grow smaller and smaller and yet being able to see more and more.

Beside him, Aurelia smiled and gazed out over the countryside. "Isn't it marvelous?"

"Marvelous," he agreed.

The view *was* marvelous — he had never considered what his estate would look like from above. But actually he was far more interested in the glowing face and sparkling eyes of the woman beside him.

She wet a finger and raised it to test the wind. He felt a sudden constriction in his chest and restrained an urge to catch hold of some part of her person. No need to be ninnyheaded about this. She was not going to fall out of this balloon as she had fallen out of the oak. Still, one never knew. He moved a little closer.

They stood in companionable silence while the balloon rose slowly higher. He tried to keep his eyes on the countryside, but she was a far more fetching sight — flushed and excited, her bonnet perched precariously on her yellow curls.

And when she turned to ask him something and her arm brushed his, he found he could not help himself. He reached out to steady her, and the next instant he was holding her in his arms.

He was a man. And he did what any man would do. He kissed her.

Her lips were soft, pliant, and her body fit perfectly against his own. A heady sensation came over him. For one wild moment he felt he might be capable of flying without the aid of the balloon.

But he made himself put her from him. Another few seconds and he would be irretrievably lost. There were still questions to be settled. And there was such a thing as propriety.

She looked up at him, those great dark eyes full of anxiety. "Milord, I . . ."

He was hard put not to kiss her again, to tell her he . . .

But common sense restrained him. "Isn't that the tradition?" he inquired, giving her his most charming smile.

She looked confused. "Tradition? What tradition?"

"That on a balloon flight a man should be kissed."

"I . . ."

The little innocent really couldn't tell he was teasing her. He'd forgotten she wasn't used to the *ton*'s ways. "I'm bamming you again," he explained. "Though I think it would be a nice tradition? Don't you?"

Aurelia, trying to contend with her pounding heart and a strange feeling of lassitude that made her want to sink into his arms, managed to smile. "Yes, milord. I suppose so. But since there aren't many female aeronauts, it might be a little difficult to achieve."

He shrugged. How, Aurelia wondered, did the tailor get his coat to fit so precisely? It was hardly the time to be thinking of coats and tailors. But how could she think of that kiss? Of being held in his arms?

If she let her thoughts go in that direction, she would move right back into his arms. And Lady Incognita's heroines never behaved like that. Not before the heroes had declared themselves.

So she remained where she was and contented herself with watching him look out at the scenery while she considered whether or not Phoebe should be apprised of this new development in the progress of The Plan.

Phoebe tossed her head. She'd been eyeing Aurelia strangely since their return from the meadow.

"Something has happened," Phoebe exclaimed. "I can see it in your face."

Aurelia felt herself coloring. Why must she give herself away? Why couldn't she just appear unconcerned?

"The Plan," Phoebe said. "You did something to advance The Plan."

Aurelia shook her head. "I did not do anything." Honesty — and friendship — compelled her to go on. "But . . . but something did happen."

"I knew it!" Phoebe rummaged in the desk drawer for the copy of *The Dark Stranger*. "Oh, do tell me."

"He . . . he kissed me."

"Kissed you?" Phoebe clasped the book to her breast and twirled round the room. "Wonderful! Marvelous!" She gazed raptly at Aurelia. "It was wonderful, wasn't it?"

Aurelia nodded. "Oh yes. I . . . I cannot say how wonderful."

Phoebe pulled out the desk chair and

opened the ink bottle. "At last something to record!"

"Phoebe . . ."

"Oh, do not look at me like that. I'm using a code. See . . . *E* equals embrace. *K* equals kiss." She turned a smiling face to her friend. "And *M* equals matrimony."

Aurelia tried to be sensible. "We must not hope too much." She said the sobering words, but she could not feel them. Her heart wanted to sing and her lips to smile. There was only the rather abrupt way he had put her from him to mar the joy of the afternoon. That, and the fact that there had been just the one kiss.

Patience, she counseled herself and turned to Phoebe. "Shall we . . ."

But Phoebe was obviously off in a day-dream. Her eyes were cloudy with emotion and her lips pursed in a strange smile. Suddenly she threw down the quill. "Aurelia, we must *do* something."

Startled, Aurelia replied, "Do something? About what?"

"About me. And your cousin."

Phoebe jumped up from the desk and began to pace the carpet.

"I thought things were going well with you," Aurelia said. "You did not come to words today?"

Phoebe laughed, a trifle shrilly. "Words? With Harold? Of course not." She stopped her pacing for a moment. "It's just that he's so abominably slow."

Aurelia smiled. "I'm afraid he would not appreciate being called slow."

"Oh, not about most things." Phoebe glanced down at Lady Incognita's book, then up at her friend. "Only about me."

"But in such a short time . . ."

"I know, I know."

If Phoebe hadn't looked so desperate, Aurelia might have laughed. As it was, she understood her friend's distress. "Please," she said. "Give Harold some more time. He *is* very shy."

Phoebe's eyes lit on the book. "That's it!" she cried. "I need A Plan."

"But Phoebe, I'm not even sure The Plan is working."

"He kissed you, didn't he?"

"Yes, but . . ."

"Well, then it's working. Now, how can I be rescued? You said Harold doesn't ride, so horses are definitely out. *I* can't climb trees, so sliding into his arms is out."

She plopped onto the velvet chaise and stared at the ceiling. "A villain, a villain. My kingdom for a villain."

Aurelia burst into laughter. "Oh, Phoebe,

I am sorry. But you are so . . . so dramatic. And surely Mr. Shakespeare would not appreciate your taking such liberties with his words."

Phoebe smiled. "He would understand, I'm sure. But where can I uncover a villain?"

"My dear, please be reasonable. This is 1819. We are no longer at war. We have no French spies. No smugglers. No pirates."

"No pirates," Phoebe repeated, looking thoughtful. "No pirates." She sat up. "That's it! The Pirates' Cave."

"What about it?"

"Harold shall rescue me."

Aurelia frowned. All the excitement — or perhaps Ranfield's kiss — had dulled her wits. "I don't know what you're talking about. How can you need to be rescued from the cave?"

"Because I shall be trapped there. By the rising tide." Phoebe got to her feet and began to prance around the room. "It will work. I know it will work. I shall be Mrs. Harold Amesley."

"The cave is dreadfully damp," Aurelia pointed out.

Phoebe shrugged. "I shan't be there long. Only long enough to be rescued. It's delightfully scary, you know. So I shall be suitably frightened. And cast myself into his arms."

"Yes," said Aurelia thoughtfully. With Phoebe in his arms, Harold might well be brought to the question. "But how shall we arrange it?"

Chapter
Twelve

It took a full week. Work on the balloons was going on apace, and it was difficult to get away. But late the next Wednesday, the young women left for a walk.

They reached the seashore in good time and made their way down to the cave. Phoebe squinted at the sun. "We shall wait until the tide comes in more. Then you can start back."

"We should wait longer," Aurelia pointed out. "Till you are really trapped. Otherwise Ranfield might find us out."

Phoebe nodded. "You're right, of course. Well, while we are waiting, let us enjoy the sea."

They took off their half boots and stockings and frolicked at the water's edge. Then, tired from the long walk and unexpected play, they sank down on the sand. It was soft and warm. Aurelia's eyes drifted shut.

She was awakened by someone shaking

her. "Hurry," Phoebe urged. "We fell asleep."

Still half-groggy, Aurelia struggled to her feet and splashed after Phoebe into the cave's mouth.

Phoebe led the way around the bend into the cave's dark recesses. "We were exploring," she said, reviewing the story they meant to tell. "First we stopped here, then there."

Aurelia tried to clear her head of the fog of sleep. The change from warm sunshine to cool dimness set her to shivering, but her thoughts were still hazy.

Finally, she roused herself to ask, "Must we go so far?"

"I suppose not," Phoebe said. "But our plan was to say that I turned my ankle and you could not bring me out."

"Yes." Aurelia tried to stop shivering. "I know The Plan. But Phoebe, are you sure . . . ? It's extremely damp in here. I shouldn't want you to take sick."

Phoebe chuckled. "I shall not take sick, I assure you. And once I cast myself into Harold's arms . . ."

Aurelia turned. "Then I suppose I had better start back." The prospect of being in the sunshine again was comforting.

Phoebe shivered. "I . . . I'll come with

you. I can say I limped that far."

They hurried back around the bend to the entrance. "Oh no!" Aurelia stopped, her bare toes curling against the cold rock. Where the entrance should be there was only water.

"It can't be!" Phoebe's wail echoed eerily through the cave. "The tide's already come in."

A space of daylight showed above the water, but only a space. And it was getting even smaller. Aurelia tried to remember how far above their heads the rocks had been when they came in. But she could not.

"Can you swim?" she asked.

Phoebe shook her head. "Of course not. Can you?"

Aurelia sighed. "No."

"What will we do?"

"There's nothing we can do."

"But . . . but they don't know where we are."

"We don't have to be rescued, you know. We'll just wait till morning and walk out."

"Au-re-li-a!"

"Phoebe, dear. Theatrics are of no use now. There's only you and I. So we must make the best of it."

"The best! I'm cold. I'm wet. I don't want to be here."

Aurelia took a deep breath. She must not

allow Phoebe to panic. She took her friend firmly by the shoulders. "Phoebe, listen. We can handle this. If we just keep our heads."

She stared into the other's frightened eyes until Phoebe nodded. "Yes, yes. Tell me what to do."

Aurelia looked around, assessing the situation. They were not in mortal danger — a flaming balloon, now that was danger. But they probably were in for a most uncomfortable night.

"First, we shall find a warm dry place."

"In here?"

"Up there on the ledge. We'll sit together." Phoebe followed her and obediently settled beside her. "Now, we'll tuck our feet under our gowns."

"Mine's wet."

"I know. Mine, too. But they will dry."

Phoebe shivered. "It's such a long time till morning."

"I know. But it will pass. And we have each other. We'll tell stories. We'll be fine."

They were not fine. As the daylight faded, the cave grew darker and colder. The drip of distant water took on ominous overtones, and the lapping of waves against the rocks below them turned sinister.

Phoebe shivered against her. "I wish I had

my India shawl. And I wish it were not so dark. And so co . . . old."

"I know, dear. I wish the same."

"Aurelia, talk to me. Tell me about ballooning. In the sun. Against the bright blue sky."

Phoebe sounded perilously close to tears, and Aurelia set her mind to making her friend feel better. But far too soon her supply of stories was exhausted.

Darkness had come down in earnest. The thin sliver of light at the top of the entrance disappeared. The darkness surrounded them, a palpable heaviness.

"Aurelia?"

"Yes?"

"Do you suppose there's any truth in them?"

"In what?"

"In the books we've been reading."

"Well, I suppose there could be."

"You mean . . . p-p-parts of dead men could be made to live?"

Aurelia swallowed a laugh. Trust Phoebe to think of Mrs. Shelley's book at a time like this. "Of course not, you goose. I thought you were talking about Lady Incognita's work."

"Oh." There was a long silence. Then, "What about ghosts?"

"What about them?" Aurelia kept her voice firm. Phoebe was in no condition to appreciate her friend's laughter.

"Do you think . . . they're . . . real?"

She saw where Phoebe's mind was headed. And she didn't like it. "I'm not positive, of course. But I imagine most stories are just that — stories people have thought up to amuse themselves. Or frighten their friends."

"But the pirates' story is true!"

Aurelia reached for patience and found it in short supply. She, too, was cold, hungry, and tired. To say nothing of wet. The last thing she needed was to be thinking of ghosts and dead pirates.

But Phoebe was her friend, so she scraped together a little more patience and said in a quiet tone, "Think now. The story has been around for many years. Ranfield said so."

Saying his name filled her with yearning. If only he would come . . . Not because she was frightened, but because she longed to see him. And she was beginning to worry about Phoebe. "What did you tell your mama before we left?"

"Only that we were going for a walk. Why?"

"I just wondered." If they had mentioned their destination, there might have been some possibility of rescue. But, since no one knew where they had gone, that seemed highly unlikely.

"Do you think . . . they might find us?"

Aurelia was torn between telling her friend the truth and keeping her spirits up. She decided for truth, uncomfortable as it was. "I don't really think so, dear. But we shall be fine. Morning will come. The tide will go out. And we will laugh over this."

In the darkness Phoebe's sigh sounded immense. "I don't think I shall ever laugh again."

"Nonsense." Aurelia forced her tone to briskness. Phoebe's tendency to the dramatic could become contagious, and she had no intention of spending an entire night shivering in unnecessary terror.

"I know," she said. "Why don't you sleep?"

"Sleep! Oh, I should like to. But I am far too cold."

"Come," said Aurelia. "Lean against me and try. It will make morning come quicker."

"Anything for that," sighed Phoebe.

With some twisting and turning, they got her curled against Aurelia's side.

"Now," Aurelia instructed, "close your eyes and relax."

"I'm trying."

Aurelia willed herself to breathe slowly and calmly. Gradually the rhythm of Phoebe's breathing slowed to match. And eventually Aurelia knew that her friend slept.

Huddled there, her arm around Phoebe, Aurelia had to struggle to keep her eyes open. She was frightfully tired herself, but she should stay awake. Though for what reason, she could not say. They were not likely to fall off the ledge, and, in spite of Phoebe's fears, there was nothing in the cave that might harm them. Slowly Aurelia's eyes closed.

The dream was patently a dream. She kept telling herself so while the cave grew lighter and lighter. Moonbeams gilded the surface of the dark water, and spirits, airy and ephemeral, fluttered from ripple to ripple, their laughter like the tinkling of tiny bells. She was about to wake Phoebe to see this wonder, when, from the surface of the shimmering sea, shot a giant hand.

"No!" The cry was torn from her throat. Her eyes flew open.

The cave was no longer dark. The moon had found a crack in the rocks above, and the cave's interior shimmered in half-light.

Phoebe stirred. "What is it?" she mumbled.

Aurelia sighed. "I had a nightmare. I saw . . ."

Her words turned into a shriek. Right before her horrified gaze, rising up out of the dark water, came a human hand!

It was followed closely by the rest of Ranfield's body. He pulled himself up and stood, towering over them. Water ran down his bared chest, dripping off his inexpressibles, and fell past his bare feet to the floor of the ledge.

Aurelia stared. Was this an apparition or reality? She had never before seen a man in such a state of undress. It so unsettled her mind that her tongue clung to the roof of her mouth.

"So," Ranfield said, and his voice rang like doom in the close confines of the cave. "You *are* here."

She managed to make her tongue work a little. "Y . . . yes."

"Are you injured?"

"I . . . no."

"Then what are you doing here?"

Phoebe made a strange noise. "We fell asleep."

Ranfield stared. "In here?"

Phoebe shook her head. "Oh no, in the sunshine outside. Then we came in to explore. And . . . and . . ."

Aurelia finished the sentence. "And the tide trapped us." She didn't like that glowering look on his face.

"You have frightened us all half to death."

"Harold!" Phoebe cried. "Where is Harold?"

"He's waiting outside. In the boat." The Earl smiled darkly, and Aurelia shivered from quite another cause than the cold. "It seems he cannot swim."

"Oh," whispered Phoebe.

Aurelia couldn't help it. The laughter came from deep within her. It rolled out, half choking her. Even if The Plan had gone right in the beginning, it would still have not succeeded. The boat could not get in. Harold could not swim.

The laughter came and came. She tried to stop it. She wanted to stop it. But she was powerless.

Ranfield jerked her to her feet. She was soaking wet. Under his hands her flesh was icy. "It's not funny." He'd been scared out of his wits, and now the chit was laughing. He'd half a mind to . . . Hysterical. Her laughter was hysterical. "Aurelia, stop. You're all right."

But still she kept on laughing. "Aurelia, stop it."

"You must slap her face," Phoebe advised. "That will . . ."

He glared at her. "One more stupidity like that and I'll never buy you another romance of terror." She subsided with a little whimper.

Now he was really doing it up brown. Threatening defenseless women. The woman he was holding continued to laugh. "Aurelia," he begged. "Please, stop."

Finally, in desperation he pulled her close to him. She was already nearly as wet as he. And maybe the heat of his body or the comfort of his arms . . . He hoped they were a comfort to her.

Gradually, her laughter slowed and stopped. But he was in no hurry to push her away. Standing there, with her body against his, he could imagine . . .

"I . . . I am recovered now." Her voice was muted. He could feel her lips against his bare chest, surprisingly warm lips.

"Good." The gentle tone of his voice surprised even him. "Because now we must get you out of here."

"Get us out?"

"Yes. I've brought a rope." He untied it from around his waist. "I mean to tie it to you and then to me. I shall swim out and pull you."

"Under the water?" Phoebe squealed.

He gave her his darkest frown. "Unless you wish to wait here till morning and the tide goes down."

"No, no."

"Fine. Then I shall proceed."

He reached for Aurelia, but she backed away. "No, take Phoebe first."

He snorted. Stubborn to the end. Well, the thing to do was get them out. And then there were going to be some explanations. He didn't for a minute believe that Bambury tale of theirs.

"Wait," said Phoebe. "Isn't the rope long enough to pass around you? In the middle. Then you could tie one of us to either end. And take us both together."

It wasn't a bad idea. He didn't like leaving either of them in the cave. And Harold waited outside. In a boat with blankets.

"Fine. Come here then."

Aurelia stood quietly while he knotted the rope around her waist. The touch of his warm hands made her shiver in quite another way than did the cold. She was over that silly laughter, and she could have waited by herself. But she was inordinately glad that it wouldn't be necessary.

He was so strong and so brave. And this was very like one of Lady Incognita's stories.

"You will have to hold your breath," he told them. "But not till we go underwater. First, we'll wade to the entrance."

Phoebe squealed as she hit the cool water. Then his warm hands closed around Aurelia's waist, and he lifted her down. She longed to put her arms around his neck, but of course she didn't. Instead she made herself concentrate on keeping her footing in the sand and rocks beneath her bare feet.

"Now," he said, offering them both a hand. "Let's go."

Aurelia had never been in water higher than her ankles. Now, as it rose to her knees, to her waist, to her breast, she found she was not frightened. *He* was there. And she trusted him.

"Now," he said. "We're going through here. Take a deep breath and hold it till we reach the other side. Try to kick your feet. That will help me."

Just before the water covered her head, Aurelia heard Phoebe gasp. Then she was being pulled along. She kicked her feet and thought of being in his arms.

And then, blessedly, she felt herself going up. Her head broke the surface of the water. And there was Harold, grinning from ear to ear and stretching out his hands to Phoebe.

With much pushing and shoving, the Earl hoisted each of them over the side. With Harold's help, he pulled himself in. Soon the rope was untied, and they were being wrapped in blankets.

Aurelia sighed. A delicious warmth was beginning to steal over her. She looked up. The Earl was still bare chested. Little droplets of water glistened on his skin. She struggled to sit up and was rewarded with a scowl. Still, she persisted. "Ranfield, you must have a blanket."

"Nonsense. I'm not cold. Now lie quiet."

Obediently she lay back. If she could just go to sleep. But he was glowering so.

"Harold," said Phoebe from the mound of blankets beside her. "How did you know where to find us?"

"Your mama said you went for a walk," Harold replied. "And Ranny remembered your fascination with the cave. And, since we couldn't find you anywhere else, we came. And here you were." He sounded mightily pleased with himself.

And Phoebe, sounding pleased, too, repeated, "Yes, here we were."

The Earl snorted. "Two of the most empty-headed chits it's ever been my misfortune to know."

Aurelia sighed again. He was being most

unfair. This time it really wasn't her fault. But of course she couldn't tell him that. For Phoebe's sake, she had to keep up the fiction they'd concocted.

"Whatever possessed you to do such a foolish thing?" he demanded.

Since he was looking right at her, Aurelia knew she had to answer. She swallowed. "I . . . I don't know. I'm truly sorry to have put you to so much trouble."

"You always are."

The grimness of his tone and the sternness of his expression made her almost wish to be back in the cave, even though it might be cold and wet and exceedingly uncomfortable. She had made him terribly angry, and all for naught. Phoebe's plan had gone horribly awry. There would be no casting into Harold's arms tonight.

But Aurelia found herself almost too tired to care. She sighed once more and let the comfort of sleep overtake her.

Chapter

Thirteen

The next morning found them no worse for their adventure. But back in the meadow, ready for another series of ascensions. Aurelia was much on edge. The Earl had not persisted in his questions the night before. He had simply carried her up the stairs and unceremoniously dumped her in her room. Mrs. Esterhill, accompanied by fluttering maids, had scurried back and forth between her room and Phoebe's until the two were tucked in warm and cozy.

But *he* had not returned, and, tired as she was, she had spent a fitful night.

This morning had been but little better. Phoebe was down in spirits because she had lost her opportunity to cast herself into Harold's arms. Uncle Arthur was so preoccupied that he barely spoke a word to anyone. And the Earl was distant and coldly polite. Only Harold was his usual self.

"I must have a chance to go up with

Harold," Phoebe whispered, her tone urgent.

Aurelia shook her head. "I can arrange nothing for you. You see how the Earl is with me."

"What's next on The Plan?"

"No!" The servants looked their way and Aurelia lowered her voice, "No more rescues."

"But how shall you bring him to the sticking point?"

"I don't know. But I cannot bear to have him so angry with me."

Phoebe smiled. "Don't worry about it. Ranfield's not one to hold a grudge. Please, will you suggest to Harold . . . ?"

"Hush. They're coming."

The approaching men were a study in contrast. Harold's clothes always looked like he'd rushed into them without sufficient thought. His rumpled appearance combined with his unruly red hair and cheerful open smile made him look friendly and accessible. As, indeed, he was.

The Earl, on the other hand, looked his usual impeccably dressed self. His dark handsomeness was enhanced by a cool politeness and a smile that never reached his eyes. But in this mood, he was enough to frighten any sensible person. At least, he frightened her.

"So," Harold said, rubbing his hands together. "Time for another flight. You all set, Reely?"

"Yes. I . . ."

A cough from Phoebe brought her words stumbling to a halt. "That is . . . I'm not feeling as well as I might." She flushed as the Earl turned to survey her. "Maybe you should take someone else. The Earl. Or Phoebe."

"Oh, Har— Mr. Amesley. I should love to go."

Harold frowned. "You won't be afraid?"

"Oh, no! Not with you."

Harold's chest seemed to expand another inch. "Well, if it's all right with Ranny."

"Ranfield? Oh, please. Please let me go."

The Earl's frown deepened. "Are you sure . . . ?"

"Oh, quite."

He shrugged. "Very well. But only a short flight. I want you back here soon."

Minutes later, Phoebe and Harold floated aloft. The workmen went about their other tasks, and Aurelia, her eyes on the balloon, was extremely conscious of the Earl beside her.

The silence between them grew. "You do think she'll be all right," he said finally.

"Who? Phoebe? Yes, yes. Of course." She

pulled nervously at the lace that edged her sleeve. It was awkward being with this distant man. She didn't know how to respond to him.

"Are you sure *you're* all right? Would you like to sit down?"

Was that real concern in his voice or was he merely playing the proper host? "I . . . I am a little tired. That is all."

"And Phoebe wanted to go aloft."

She had been staring after the receding balloon. Now she forced herself to meet his eyes. Their brilliance was clouded. "Yes," she said. "Phoebe wanted to go aloft."

For a moment she considered swooning into his arms. But the way he was acting, he might well become even angrier. And besides, never having swooned, she didn't know if she could carry it off.

His face darkened. "Why should a female wish to risk life and limb in such pursuits?"

Was he questioning her motives or Phoebe's? "It depends. Phoebe has found the idea exciting ever since you first mentioned it. And now . . ."

"And now," he finished for her, his eyes compelling. "She has a *tendre* for Harold."

"Perhaps."

He didn't question her answer. "And you?"

"I simply love to be aloft."

He frowned. "In a wicker basket. With a brazier full of fire."

She smiled. "Really, milord. It is not that dangerous. The brazier is suspended, you know. There's always plenty of water in case something should catch. And, besides, with our balloon there is no fire."

Ranfield shrugged. He was still upset over last night's episode. The emotions that had wracked him when Aurelia was found missing had been so intense and his relief on finding her so exhilarating that he'd had the most difficult time not declaring himself then and there. But for Phoebe, he would probably have silenced Aurelia's laughter with another kiss. And been irrevocably lost.

But a night of sober reflection and very little sleep had convinced him that Providence, and Phoebe's presence, had saved him from a great mistake. It was foolhardy to marry such a woman — great dark eyes and rosebud mouth notwithstanding.

She raised those eyes to him and asked, "Do you know why Napoleon did not use balloons to attack England?"

He conquered a desire to laugh — not at her, but at himself. While he was wrestling with knotty problems, she was, as usual, contemplating ballooning.

"I believe that at one time he made such plans," he replied.

"I wonder why he didn't follow through on them. Though of course I'm glad he didn't. Victory might then have gone to the other side."

Balloons, he thought sourly. With her it was always balloons. "I believe I read about it. When he was crowned emperor, they sent up a balloon. And it went off course and came down in Rome, punctured by Nero's tomb, or some such thing. And Boney was insulted, felt people were laughing at him. So he closed down his ballooning school and gave up his plans to invade us by air."

"Vanity," she mused. "His vanity made him give up what could have brought him victory."

To his surprise he found himself teasing a little. "You sound disappointed."

Her cheeks turned pink and her eyes sparkled. "Oh, no! I was only thinking that he missed a great opportunity."

"Of course." He studied her face. Why could talking to her — and about balloons, always about balloons — make him feel so much better? It was not sensible. Still, he went on doing it. "No doubt you've heard

185

about the combination balloon — the *charlo-montgolfière* — with a hydrogen bag above for the primary lift and a hot-air balloon suspended below to regulate altitude. I understand it eliminates the need for sand ballast."

She nodded. "Yes, but that one *is* dangerous."

He could hardly believe his ears. "It is?"

"Of course. To have a fire so close to the gas is inviting trouble. It can be done, of course. But I should not care to do it."

Why should that simple statement make him feel so relieved? He had already decided marriage to her was out of the question. "You shouldn't?"

"I shouldn't. I wish to fly," she explained sweetly. "Not to be incinerated."

"One lump, please." Aurelia smiled as Phoebe solemnly poured the tea. Since their return from the meadow, Phoebe's eyes had glowed. But whatever had transpired up there in the gondola had certainly dulled her other faculties. She had almost missed the cup once, and now she had forgotten everyone's preferences.

Aurelia sipped her tea and leaned back in the chair. Across the room, Ranfield was deep in conversation with Uncle Arthur.

And on Phoebe's other side sat an enthralled Harold, his teacup forgotten.

Aurelia sipped in contentment. It was good to have the Earl more like his usual self. There seemed still some constraint between them, but it had lessened after their talk in the meadow.

"It was wonderful," Phoebe said to Harold, her eyes saying much more.

Harold nodded in satisfaction. "Yes, it's like I told you. Nothing's better than going aloft. Unless it's . . ." His voice fell away to a murmur, and Phoebe's face grew pinker.

Whatever had happened up there seemed to have advanced Phoebe's cause. There was little doubt that Harold would be brought to the question. But why must men be so infernally slow about these things?

Aurelia glanced across the room to where Ranfield leaned against the mantel. Would he ever ask . . . ?

"Phoebe!" Cousin Prudence hurried into the room, her cap askew, her spectacles on the very end of her nose.

"Yes, Mama?"

"I have just heard the most terrible news." She fixed Harold with a scowl, and he focused all his attention on the delicate Wedgwood cup in his hand.

Phoebe's face paled. "What is it, Mama?"

"I just heard that you have been up in that . . . that Devil's contrivance! My own daughter, my own little girl, sailing about in the heavens! Oh, I can't bear it! How could you? How could you do such a thing to me?"

"Oh, Mama. I didn't do it *to you.* I did it *for me.* It's so beautiful up there. You can see so far. All of God's beauties are . . ."

"Stop!" Cousin Prudence's face grew redder, and her cap threatened to topple from her head. Hands on hips, she glared at Harold. "It was you!" she cried. "You . . . you . . . popinjay. You tarnished my little girl's soul with your wicked talk."

Aurelia bit her bottom lip. It was unkind to laugh at the woman's obvious distress. But the idea of Harold as a popinjay . . . Or even of him tarnishing souls . . .

"If I were a man, I should have you horse-whipped," Cousin Prudence went on.

Harold paled, but held his ground. "I say, ma'am, there's no need to go into such a taking. Why, Phoebe was safe up there with me. Safe . . . safe as she is sitting here in this drawing room."

"Safe!" Cousin Prudence's voice rose several octaves.

The Earl turned and crossed the room. "You must not blame Harold," he told his cousin. "They asked my permission, and I gave it."

Cousin Prudence was obviously torn between her desire to speak her mind and her obligation to the kinsman who had provided for her. "It's not right," she muttered finally. "The Good Lord didn't mean for people to fly. If he had, there'd be mention of it in the Good Book."

Uncle Arthur crossed the room. He rubbed his bald pate. "Excuse me, Mrs. Esterhill. But are those spectacles you're wearing?"

She eyed him as though he'd lost his reason. "Of course they're spectacles."

Uncle Arthur smiled, the smile of a cat ready to pounce. "I should like to remind you that spectacles are not mentioned in the Scriptures."

Cousin Prudence snorted. "Course not. They didn't have 'em then."

Aurelia pulled in a breath. Uncle Arthur had her fairly trapped.

"Then why are you wearing them?"

"I need 'em to see." Cousin Prudence stared at him. "I know what you're getting at," she said at last. "But spectacles . . . that's a different thing than flying about in the skies. Spectacles help people."

"So does air flight."

Cousin Prudence shook her head. "You'll never make me believe that." She looked at the Earl, her gaze accusing. "To think that you'd permit such goings on."

"I'm sorry, cousin, that you're offended." The Earl's tone was kindly, but firm, the tone of a man accustomed to obedience. And quite sure that he was right. "I saw no danger in Phoebe's going up. She was well attended. No harm came of it."

"No . . ." The look on the Earl's dark face made Cousin Prudence swallow the rest of her sentence. "Yes, milord," she murmured. "If you'll excuse me, I have dinner to see to."

Then she was gone, buzzing out like an angry bee.

"Now you're in the suds," the Earl said to Phoebe.

She smiled. "I cannot help it. I cannot give up air flight. It's so wonderful. Oh, Ranfield, what can we do to make Mama understand?"

He shook his head. "I do not know, Phoebe. I really do not know."

Chapter

Fourteen

"But, Aurelia, I am not imagining this." Phoebe turned from the window where a heavy rain beat against the casement.

Aurelia considered her friend. The constant rain had set them all on edge, giving everyone gloomy faces and drooping shoulders. "I don't see that much difference in your mama's ways."

Phoebe frowned. "She is so much quieter. And she doesn't expound on the Scriptures nearly so much."

Aurelia patted her friend's hand. "Perhaps all this rain has been too much for her."

Phoebe shook her head. "No, it's not the rain. It's something else. I've never seen her this way before. Never."

Aurelia sighed. Phoebe was getting more and more difficult, She could sympathize with her friend's impatience. Two more weeks had passed, and Harold, though he was attentive, had still not come up to snuff. And Ranfield . . .

Aurelia would never understand the man. One minute he was all charm and wit, and the next he was cold and distantly polite. Such erratic behavior was very unnerving. She found herself almost as up and down in her spirits as was her friend.

"Well," said Phoebe, throwing herself on the chaise. "I don't know what to do about it. But I assure you, something is wrong."

Aurelia frowned. "She is your mama, and you know her much better than I do. So I will have to take your word for it." She looked around the room. "Shall we go downstairs or shall we read aloud?"

Phoebe sighed. "Let's read aloud. The men are off somewhere." She shoved a pillow under her head. "Something about rigging, I believe. And I'd rather avoid Mama for the present."

"Very well. Shall we finish Mrs. Shelley's *Frankenstein*?"

"Yes." Phoebe settled herself comfortably. But Aurelia had only just picked up the book when Phoebe jumped to her feet. "I can't do it," she cried. "I simply can't do it!"

"Can't do what?"

"I can't let you forget about The Plan."

Aurelia frowned. "I told you. I don't want to hear any more about it."

"But one final rescue . . . That's all you need. I'm sure we could arrange it."

"Phoebe." Aurelia looked her friend straight in the eye. "Listen to me carefully. His last rescue of us nearly cost me the Earl's friendship. He's only just getting back to his usual self."

"But you know it's always after the last and biggest rescue that the hero declares himself."

Aurelia drew herself up. It didn't make her any taller than Phoebe, but she hoped it impressed her friend. "Phoebe, I mean what I say. No more rescues."

Phoebe sighed. "Very well. But with two balloons . . ."

"Phoebe!"

Phoebe stopped before her, her eyes pleading. "Please, just listen to me. It's a perfect Pl— It's perfect. You challenge him to a race. His hot-air balloon against your gas one. You both go up. You have difficulties and come down. He comes down after you, rescues you, and asks the question."

Aurelia shook her head. "No, no, and no! One more rescue and the Earl will send me back to London."

Phoebe tossed her curls. "Well, it's an excellent Plan. I cannot for the life of me see why you want to forsake it."

Aurelia made no reply. She had already explained herself in great detail — and more than once. There remained nothing more to be said.

Phoebe took another turn around the room. "Oh, Aurelia, it's just so aggravating. I know Harold wants to ask me, but I can't get him to do it."

Aurelia opened the book. "Patience, Phoebe. However hard it is, we must have patience." And, feeling that she would never really be patient again, she began to read.

Downstairs, the Earl shook the rain from his hair and sank into a chair. His eyes lit on the Turner painting above the mantel. What interesting effects the man could achieve working with sunlight on water. He frowned. But fond as he was of painting, at the moment he was far more interested in the effects of sunlight on a certain golden head.

Her hair gleamed like — burnished gold. His frown deepened. He disliked the avaricious element of the comparison. Aurelia Amesley and gold were far different. Aurelia was warm and giving. Gold was cold and uncaring. But, he reminded himself, gold was, at least, stable. It did not . . .

"Ranny? You got a minute?"

Aurelia's cousin paused in the doorway, his face all anxiety.

"Yes, Harold. Come in."

Harold came in, but he seemed unable to stand still. He fidgeted first on one foot and then on the other. He pulled at his waistcoat and then on his cuffs.

"Yes?" Ranfield asked.

"I . . . Ah . . ."

"For heaven's sake man, get on with it."

"It's . . . It's Phoebe."

Ranfield swallowed a chuckle. So Harold had at last been brought to the question. "Yes?"

"I . . . We . . . That is . . . Confound it, Ranny. How do I ask her?"

Ranfield pretended ignorance. "Ask her what?"

"You know. Be my wife and all that."

Ranfield allowed himself a small smile. "You just ask her. And forget about the all that."

"But . . . But what if she says no?"

Ranfield adjusted his cuff. "You'll never know till you've tried."

Harold paled, his freckles standing out. " 'Fraid I'm doing this all wrong. Ought to be asking your permission, not your directions."

Ranfield chuckled. "It's all right, Harold. I don't imagine you have much practice at this sort of thing."

Harold's eyes widened. "Practice! Lord, no! Never thought of getting hitched before. Wouldn't think of it now, except . . ."

Ranfield sighed. "Except you can't think about living without her."

Harold grinned. "By Jove. How'd you know?"

Ranfield smoothed his cravat. "The symptoms of love are common, Harold. They afflict everyone in the same way."

Harold nodded. "Spose so. Though it don't seem likely anyone else could feel this good." He paused. "There's one thing bothers me though. Her mama . . . She don't like me one bit."

Ranfield frowned. That was true enough. Cousin Prudence was going to fly up in the boughs about this. And calming her would be a tricky business.

Harold yanked at his waistcoat again. "She can't stop us, can she?"

"No, Harold. I'm Phoebe's guardian. But give her mama some time. Try to get her to come round."

He was afraid it was going to take more time than any of them had, but Harold could at least try.

"So, when are you planning to ask Phoebe?"

"I ain't sure. Soon as I can get my nerve up."

Ranfield nodded. "Good."

"But if she says no . . ."

"It's best to know the truth."

"Spose you're right," Harold said, turning to leave. "Spose you're right."

The Earl sighed. Too bad he wasn't intelligent enough to take his own advice. Was it really because of Aurelia's mishaps that he had put off asking her? After all, those did seem to be over. Or was it because he was afraid to hear her answer?

It hardly seemed possible that she would turn him down. But there was that statement she'd made that day in the *Minerva* when she'd told him quite plainly that she didn't desire his company. And she did not give him any of the signals he was accustomed to getting from women. He could cope with society misses who said one thing and meant quite another. He could easily interpret their sighs and smiles, their fluttering lashes and downcast eyes.

But Aurelia was different. There was no artifice about her. From her a friendly smile was just that — a friendly smile. And yet it could mean much. Or it could mean nothing. And he was forever trying to figure it out.

He frowned and got to his feet. Botheration! He should bring himself to the sticking point. Ask the question and have done with it.

But when they gathered in the drawing room for tea later that afternoon, he was still undecided. And, from the absence of joy on Phoebe's face, it appeared Harold had not yet gotten to the question either.

Aurelia's uncle came in and took a chair. He was beaming in satisfaction. "Good workmen you've got," he said. "Our balloon is in tiptop shape."

"When are you taking her up?"

"Tomorrow morning, if the weather clears. Harold will take her. Just for a short hop. It takes such a while to fill the balloon. Time-consuming, it is, making the hydrogen gas."

"But it's better than hot air," Aurelia said, coming into the room.

Her uncle nodded. "Of course, my dear."

And the two of them were off. Ranfield listened with half an ear. He was far more occupied with looking than with listening. Aurelia was wearing a creation of lavender and pink that set off her color admirably, and her hair was piled on her head, cascading in curls from a center part. He suppressed a longing to wrap one golden curl around his finger.

Phoebe approached him. "Ranfield?"

He tore his eyes away from Aurelia. "Yes?"

"Have you noticed anything different about Mama?"

He considered this. "No, I can't say that I have."

"Well, I have. She's acting strangely."

He gave Phoebe his attention. She really did look concerned. "Do you think she's ill?"

"I don't know. She's just strange."

Could Cousin Prudence have guessed what was coming? He didn't want to tip Harold's hand. "Perhaps it's just the press of extra work. With our guests and all."

"Perhaps," Phoebe said, but she looked doubtful.

She moved away then, back to stand by Harold. And her mama entered with the tea things.

Ranfield considered his cousin. She did not look ill. Her cheeks were their usual healthy pink, and her eyes were clear. But Phoebe was right. Her mama was not her usual self.

For one thing, she didn't move with the same brisk motion. And for another, she muttered not a single imprecation against the Devil's contrivance.

He shook his head. This rain was making them all daft. They were imagining things. Cousin Prudence was probably just having an off day.

"Come," he said, moving toward the table. "Let us have tea. Cousin Prudence, will you pour?"

Chapter

Fifteen

The next Monday, they went to the meadow so that Uncle Arthur and Harold could test the hot-air balloon. Though it meant rising very early, Phoebe and Aurelia had insisted on being included in the excursion.

Standing there, in the early morning glow, Aurelia felt the beauty of the scene around her. A light dew sprinkled the grass and sparkled on the leaves. The world was pristine and new. And beside her stood the man . . .

"They're certainly up high enough," Ranfield remarked.

Aurelia nodded. She didn't know how Harold had persuaded Uncle Arthur to let Phoebe go up. She could understand him letting her go in the hot-air balloon. After all, it was Ranfield's and fuel for it was cheap. But hydrogen gas was an expensive commodity. And Uncle Arthur was not a man given to waste.

She stifled a sigh. She had half-hoped to

go on this flight herself. A little time up there might help her, though temporarily, to forget the problems of her earthbound existence.

"Disappointed?" asked the Earl.

She turned to him. "Yes. A little. The world looks so beautiful this morning. But I am glad Phoebe will get to see it from up there."

His smile was wry. "Providing she looks."

"How could she not . . ." The memory of his arms around her, his mouth on hers, rose to her mind. She flushed and went silent. Were Harold and Phoebe kissing up there? It was hard to imagine Harold engaged in such a pursuit, especially in a balloon. But she had to admit that, though unlikely, it was possible.

"So," inquired Ranfield. "Do you still hold that gas is better than hot air?"

"Of course." She looked at him in surprise. "Why should I change my mind about a thing like that?"

"Why indeed." He looked at her closely. "Do you find that you often change your mind?"

He asked the question with such seriousness that she paused to consider her answer. "I . . . No, I suppose I do not. And assuredly not about something this important."

"I see."

He sighed and his expression was almost melancholy. Whatever was he thinking now? Surely the man couldn't be upset because she espoused hydrogen gas over hot air. She had done that all along. But then what was bothering him?

"What . . ." she was just beginning. Then down from the heavens came a great shout.

Aurelia looked skyward in alarm. Whatever could be wrong? But everything seemed in order. The balloon looked fine, and Harold and Phoebe were leaning over the side of the gondola, waving handkerchiefs. They were too far up to see their faces properly. But waving handkerchiefs was not a signal of distress.

"What are they yelling about?" Aurelia mused, only half aloud.

"I believe," said Ranfield in that dry tone he sometimes used, "that they have decided to join forces."

"Join forces?"

He nodded. "I believe Harold has just proposed marriage. But see, they are coming down and will tell us themselves."

Before the balloon was properly tethered, Phoebe was scrambling over the side. "Oh, Aurelia!" she cried. "It's happened! I'm to be Mrs. Harold Amesley."

To her complete surprise, Aurelia found

her eyes filling with tears. "How very wonderful," she said. "I'm so happy for you."

With Phoebe's arms around her, Aurelia blinked away the tears. Phoebe, at least, had achieved her ends. And no matter what, she and Aurelia would now be connected. This thought was not as comforting as she might have hoped, and she was forced to blink still more.

Then Harold was hugging her. "I'm so lucky," he said, his face one big smile. "Just think. Phoebe likes it up there. She really likes it."

Aurelia swallowed a laugh. How like Harold to think of ballooning even now. And how fortunate that Phoebe shared his interest. "I am so happy for you," she repeated. Harold hugged her again and moved away.

And then she found herself facing Ranfield. Phoebe and Harold, engrossed in hugging each other, saw nothing around them. And when the Earl stepped forward and put his arms around her, Aurelia did not demur. "A congratulatory hug seems to be in order," he whispered, "now that we are to be related."

His nearness made her quite lightheaded, and her knees had taken on a distressing tendency to go limp as a deflated balloon. "Yes," she murmured, wondering if she dared cling to him for support. But that might well be misconstrued. "Yes, it is wonderful to see them so happy."

Was she imagining it or had she actually felt his lips brush her ear? Her heart went off into a wild dance, and she struggled to keep her expression calm. Since he was now setting her from him, she must be careful not to give away her feelings. The Earl might well mean to show only friendliness. Were not *tonnish* people always kissing and embracing?

"I must ask you to hold off setting a date," the Earl said to the happy pair.

Phoebe's expression of joy vanished and Harold frowned. "Why?" he asked.

"I want you to bring Phoebe's mama round to your way of thinking. You'll have no end of trouble if you don't."

Aurelia conceded the wisdom of this. But she saw no way Cousin Prudence could be persuaded. Harold would not — could not — give up air flight. And Cousin Prudence was so strongly against it.

"So, Mama," Phoebe said some time later as they faced her mama in the kitchen. "Harold has asked me to marry him."

The two young people clung to each

other's hands. Aurelia could understand why — Cousin Prudence was no mean adversary.

For a moment after the revelation, Phoebe's mama stood stock still. Nothing about her moved, but her face grew redder and redder until Aurelia feared some sort of medical mishap.

And then the dam burst. Phoebe's mama rounded on Harold. "You misbegotten son of a . . ."

"Mama!"

Phoebe's mama swung to her. "Quiet, young woman! How dare you? You know how I feel about air flight." She shoved at the spectacles that threatened to slip off the end of her nose. "It's the work of the Devil. And you want to marry this . . . this popinjay."

Harold drew himself to his full height. "That ain't fair!" he declared. "I don't pay no mind to clothes. Reely can tell you that."

He pulled in a deep breath. "But I'll make Phoebe a good husband. Better than any. You've my word on that."

Cousin Prudence's face was now a most alarming crimson. "I forbid it!" she shouted. "I absolutely forbid such a marriage."

"Ma . . . ma!"

Phoebe's wail pierced Aurelia's heart. Where was Ranfield? Why didn't he do something?

But the Earl was nowhere in sight. Cousin Prudence jerked her cap straight, shoved her spectacles up her nose again, and declared, "Never. Never. Never!" before she stomped out, the image of outraged motherhood.

Phoebe tore her hand from Harold's and rushed to her friend. "Oh, Aurelia! Whatever shall I do?"

Aurelia was at a loss to reply. Her own mama had been of the quiet weepy species, her maternal edicts easily circumvented by appealing to Papa's authority.

Aurelia patted Phoebe's hand. "You must calm yourself, my dear. Surely the Earl will discover a way."

But the Earl did not. He seemed singularly undisposed to offer them any help. And, in sober fact, he was most of the time absent on one errand or another about the estate, so much so that they rarely saw him at all.

One day passed. Two days. A whole week.

And Cousin Prudence remained as adamant as ever. She stormed about the house, cap askew and lips tight pressed. The slightest word or look was enough to set her off.

Aurelia was only slightly less distressed than her friend and her cousin. To see the two of them moping around was heart-rending. And still the Earl did nothing.

By the end of the second week, Phoebe was beside herself. Harold was little better. Aurelia even feared letting him go up in the balloon, so preoccupied did he seem. But he went out to the shed to attend to something, and the two young women took themselves to Aurelia's room.

"We must do something," Phoebe said the minute the door closed behind them. "We must *make* Mama understand."

"I wish we could," said Aurelia sadly. "But there is no way. She simply hates air flight."

Phoebe sighed. "I know. But we must think of something. How . . . how can we get Mama's consent?"

Absently she picked up *The Dark Stranger*. They had written nothing in it since Aurelia had forsaken The Plan. But the copy still lay on her desk, a mute reminder that all had not gone well.

Phoebe paced, back and forth, clutching the book. "There is nothing for it," she said finally. "We must fly to Gretna Green."

Aurelia did not like this look in Phoebe's eyes. Such wildness could only lead to more distress.

"Now dear. You cannot do that. You must wait. The Earl said he would help."

Phoebe snorted. "Ranfield! Ranfield has done nothing. Except tell us to wait. Aurelia, I cannot wait much longer."

She dropped the book on the desk. "Oh, we have made such wonderful plans. We shall call ourselves the Aeronautical Amesleys and go up together. Oh, it will be grand." And she burst into tears.

Aurelia hurried to comfort her. "Come, dear. Sit here on the chaise beside me."

Phoebe cried for some time. Finally she raised her head. "Mama will not permit our marriage. Unless Harold gives up ballooning. You know he cannot do that. I would not ask it of him. Gretna Green is our only hope."

Aurelia shook her head. "Phoebe, dear. Scotland is a long way off. Don't you see? Someone would catch up with you long before you reached there."

Phoebe sniffled. "We must do something. Please, Aurelia, help us plan something."

Aurelia sighed. Plan, indeed. She was the last one to turn to for success in such a venture. "So far all my plans have come to naught. But let me think about it."

Another week passed, and the heat of July was fully upon them. Phoebe was wilting away. Harold, in spite of hours in the sun, grew paler.

One hot afternoon, Aurelia found Phoebe in the library. Her friend was huddled on the divan, clutching *The Dark Stranger*, and weeping copiously. Her face was all splotchy and her clothes were in disarray. Aurelia wiped the perspiration from her forehead. The weather had been truly beastly, and her own nerves were ready to ignite. "Please, Phoebe. You must stop this."

"Oh, Aurelia, I was reading. And it's just so beautiful. Such true love."

Patience, Aurelia cautioned herself. She sought the right words. "My dear, it's a story. A fiction. It's not real."

Phoebe shook her head. "No. No. It *is* real. It's exactly how I feel about Harold. And he about me."

"Oh, Phoebe. You will make yourself ill with all these tears. You must stop crying. Be brave."

Phoebe wiped at her eyes with a sodden handkerchief. "I have tried. I really have.

But if I may not marry Harold, then . . . Then I wish to die!"

"Phoebe!" Aurelia looked anxiously toward the door. "Think what your mama would have to say to such a sentiment. We should be drowned in Scriptures instead of tears."

But Phoebe could not be brought to smile. Tears continued to trickle down her cheeks. "We must do something," she insisted. "Perhaps we should go to London. To the Fleet."

Aurelia swallowed hard. Above all Phoebe must not have a Fleet marriage. She must not go to that dangerous neighborhood where an illegal marriage could be bought for very little, where unscrupulous men often brought unsuspecting women. Even Gretna Green was to be preferred to a marriage that might not be a marriage at all.

She turned away to pace the carpet before the fireplace. There must be some other way out of this situation. If only Ranfield would help. Why couldn't he make Cousin Prudence give her consent? Living on his largess as she did, she could hardly defy his authority.

"Yes," Phoebe continued. "We could be married in the Fleet. Maybe Ranfield wouldn't think to follow us there." She sniffled. "Mama will be sorry when I'm gone from her. So sorry."

Aurelia paused and stared thoughtfully into space, Phoebe's words echoing in her ears. *What if . . . ?*

"We must do something," Phoebe repeated. "Either Gretna Green or the Fleet. One or the other." She sat up suddenly, *The Dark Stranger* slipping unheeded from her grasp. "I tell you, Aurelia, I shall marry Harold. No one shall stop me."

With another hurried look at the door, Aurelia crossed the room. "Ssssh, Phoebe. You shall get married. But listen, I've just thought of something."

Phoebe turned an eager face. "Oh, tell me. Do tell me. I will do anything."

Despite the heat, Aurelia shivered. If Ranfield ever found out she'd suggested such a thing to his cousin . . . "This is The Plan."

Chapter

Sixteen

Late the next afternoon, Ranfield looked across the tea table at Aurelia. The heat had lessened somewhat, and she looked fetching in her gown of azure blue highlighted by a matching ribbon twined among her curls. He sighed. In spite of his very sensible conviction that he should keep away from all of them, and from Aurelia in particular, he had given in to the temptation to look at her face, to hear the soft tones of her voice. Perhaps to touch . . .

"So," she inquired. "Do you think linen or silk better for the manufacture of balloons?"

He swallowed another sigh. Balloons. Balloons. Always balloons. "Linen or . . ."

"Where is that confounded boy?" Arthur Amesley complained, bursting into the room. "He ought to be back by now."

Ranfield looked at Aurelia. "Now, uncle," she said. "You know these errands take time."

Her uncle nodded, but it was apparent he wasn't really hearing her words. "Didn't send him that far," he muttered. "Shouldn't have let him take the girl along with him. Probably stopped to buy her ribbons and other gewgaws."

What was the meaning of that strange expression on Aurelia's face? Something wasn't right here. "Phoebe went with him?" he asked.

Arthur Amesley nodded. "Should have been back by now."

Ranfield frowned, his eyes still on Aurelia. There was something about her look, something . . . secretive.

Cousin Prudence bustled in, cap askew. "Where is that girl? She promised to pick some flowers for me. To decorate the table for dinner."

Aurelia got to her feet with an alacrity that made her immediately more suspect in his eyes. "I'll pick them," she said. "What kind do you want?"

Ranfield watched her turn toward the French doors. He was right. She was uncommonly eager to get shut of this discussion.

"Wait!" His voice rang out louder than he intended, and they all turned to stare at him. "There's something going on here," he told her sternly. "And I mean to get to the bottom of it."

He had never seen anyone look guiltier. But his sternest look did not elicit a confession. She simply shook her head. "I don't know what you mean," she said. Obviously it was going to take more than a hard look to make her give him the truth.

He reached for the bellpull and Pratt appeared. "Send someone to Miss Phoebe's room. See if there's a note for one of us."

Another strange expression crossed Aurelia's face. Guilt? Or relief?

The silence grew. A million thoughts crossed his mind, but he voiced none of them. Shortly Pratt returned. "I found this, milord."

Ranfield ripped open the envelope that bore his name and read the note aloud.

Dear Ranfield,
We don't want to do this. But we cannot wait any longer. We've run off to be married. Please tell Mama we love each other dearly. And we love her, too.
Phoebe

"Ohhhhh!" Cousin Prudence wailed. "My poor baby! That monster has made off with my baby."

Arthur Amesley bristled. "Monster, is it?

215

You're the one that's the cause of all this. My boy loves your Phoebe. He wanted to marry her right and proper. But oh no, you wouldn't have that."

Cousin Prudence burst into tears. "Oh, Dear Lord. What have I done?"

Though Ranfield found the little drama most interesting, he was still watching Aurelia. Her surprise at hearing the note's contents had been contrived. She was such an abominably poor liar. He was convinced she had known exactly what the note would say before a word of it left his lips.

So, Phoebe and Harold were on their way to get married. What a bumble broth this was! Perhaps he should have told them. But how then could he have tested Harold's sincerity? One more week of their devotion to each other, and he had planned to elicit Cousin Prudence's consent himself. He would have preferred to have it given voluntarily, but he was not above using his authority if the occasion demanded. There would have been no problems. He usually accomplished what he set out to do.

Well, enough of that. He must do something now. "Let us be calm," he began. But Prudence pressed a hand to her brow in the exact manner of a Cheltenham tragedienne and moaned, "Oh my, I feel so faint."

And right there in front of him, she collapsed into Arthur Amesley's arms. Such a look of astonishment Ranfield had never before witnessed on a man's face. Amesley stood like stone, the limp woman clasped against his waistcoat, his face a study in consternation.

Ranfield hastened forward. Swooning women were nothing new to him. "Here, let me help you," he told the paralyzed Amesley. "Let's put her on the divan. Aurelia, ring for Pratt."

With trembling hands Aurelia turned away to pull the bell rope. Whatever had made her invent such a foolish plan? Cousin Prudence looked absolutely white. If something terrible happened to her mama, Phoebe would never forgive her.

The Earl was chafing Cousin Prudence's wrists when Pratt appeared. "Bring smelling salts," the Earl ordered. "And a cool cloth for her head."

Pratt was gone in an instant and Aurelia hurried to the couch. "What shall we do?" It was more a question to herself than to Ranfield.

But he looked up, his eyes meeting hers. She fought to keep her gaze steady. She could not let him know . . .

"She'll come round," he said, in that excessively polite tone she had learned to dislike. "Here, Prudence . . ."

Cousin Prudence sat up, her eyes wide. "Where is he?" she demanded shrilly.

Ranfield sighed. "Where is who?"

"That man."

"I'm right here." Uncle Arthur moved around so he could be seen. His face was crimson, but his expression remained resolute. "I'm sorry you took faint, ma'am. Indeed, I am. But I don't take back what I said. Not one word of it." He rubbed his head. "If you'd have let them get hitched, none of this would have happened."

Cousin Prudence drew a long shuddering breath. "You're right," she said. "You're quite right."

Outside the window a bird caroled. Inside the room there was complete silence. Aurelia could hear her own breath echoing in her ears as she stared at the woman on the divan. Turning, she saw that Ranfield and her uncle were staring, too.

"There's no call to goggle at me," Cousin Prudence declared in aggrieved tones. "I hope I can recognize the error of my ways." She moaned. "Oh, if only I'd realized sooner. My poor baby. My only child."

Two great tears rolled down her cheeks, an effect somewhat marred by the fact that her cap had fallen over one ear and gave her a decidedly rakish appearance. "I do so want to see her properly married."

"Perhaps you can," the Earl said. "If I set out right away, I may be able to overtake the culprits."

Cousin Prudence clasped her hands. "Oh, milord, would you? Would you really do that? I'd be eternally grateful."

The Earl considered this. "And you won't obstruct the marriage?"

"No, milord. No, indeed. Just bring my little girl back. I'll give them my blessing, I will. I promise before God."

Slowly Aurelia let the breath from her lungs.

The Earl regarded his cousin, his eyes stern. "And you will refrain from all railing against aeronautics?"

Aurelia gnawed at her bottom lip. This was more than they had hoped for. But they had never supposed the Earl would ask for so much. Phoebe's mama blanched, but she swallowed and said bravely, "Yes, milord. I will refrain."

"Very well," he said. "I'll have my horse saddled and be off."

He turned to Aurelia and she felt her knees go weak. "Have you any idea of their destination?"

She swallowed. When he looked at her like that, so fierce and unyielding, she knew The Plan had been nothing but a foolish dream. "I don't know for sure. I mean, I did not . . ." There was no sense in going on in that line; plainly he didn't believe she was unaware of what had happened. She pulled herself together. "I suppose . . . Well, perhaps Gretna Green . . ."

"I thought as much. Take care of Prudence. I'll be back when I've found them."

And he strode out, leaving Aurelia and her uncle staring at each other in dismay.

The road north fell away under the stallion's hooves, and Ranfield, sitting easily in the saddle, gave himself up to thought. What an addlepated scheme. And he had thought Harold a sensible fellow.

He cursed. He should have known better. What man in the throes of love was ever sensible? Look at the antics of his own mind. He who had once considered only dark willowy beauties with classic features was now captivated by a small, gamine-faced chit, with the reprehensible habit of courting disaster.

Probably her face and form had nothing to do with his feelings, though. Mama had told him that many times — that outward attributes were fine but the inward ones more important. He had laughed then, in the callowness of his green years. But now . . . He could see she was right.

Inward attributes. Well, Aurelia was loyal enough. And brave. No one had ever before stood up to his fiercest look and refused him the information he demanded. He was still convinced of her involvement in this bumble broth. Phoebe and Harold would scarcely have taken such a step without confiding in her.

But what did they hope to accomplish? The women might suppose the pair could elude him. But Harold should know better.

And that was another thing. How had they convinced Harold to undertake such a lamebrained scheme? The fellow might have little regard for the amenities of society, but where women were concerned he was a tower of respectability.

Ranfield glanced at the sinking sun. Another hour and the pair would have to stop for the night. He would find them before the darkness was well along.

Actually, it was almost three in the morning before he discovered the particular inn that housed the runaways. He satisfied himself that it was indeed they by identifying his curricle. Then he gave orders to have his horse cared for and had himself a hearty meal. By the time daylight broke, he was feeling half-human again.

Phoebe was first down the stairs. She had come to request the carriage be readied. Ranfield waited till she had spoken to the innkeeper, then he stepped from the shadows of the great room and confronted her. "Good morning, cousin."

Her face turned pale and he thought for a moment she might swoon. But she rallied. "R . . . Ranfield. How did you . . . ?"

"It wasn't difficult to guess your destination."

"Mama? What did Mama say?"

"Your mama fainted dead away."

She put a hand to her mouth. "Oh dear! Did she injure herself?"

"No. Mr. Amesley caught her."

The door above opened. "Phoebe," Harold called. "Where . . . ?"

"Harold." There was only a faint quiver in her voice. "Ranfield is come."

"Oh." Harold came down the stairs, a sheepish expression on his face. "Morning, milord."

"Good morning. Well, what have you to say for yourselves?"

He made his voice stern, but he couldn't

help feeling a certain tenderness. The two of them were such innocents.

Harold took Phoebe's hand. "We said it already. We want to be married. We tried, Ranfield. But Phoebe's mama . . . she just couldn't be brought round. And Phoebe . . ." He swallowed. "That is, *I* decided Gretna Green was our only choice."

"Didn't you know I'd catch up with you?"

Harold nodded. "Had to consider that." He dropped Phoebe's hand and stepped forward. "Deal me a facer if . . ."

"Harold! No!"

Harold turned. "Phoebe, my love. He's got a right to be angry. I'd be up in the boughs if I was him." He swung back. "So see, as I was saying, deal me a facer if you like, but I love her. And we'll persist till we get married."

A tearful Phoebe nodded.

Ranfield knew he ought to give them a good scare. But try as he would to frown, he kept wanting to smile. "You are not going to Gretna Green," he said. "Not ever."

"Begging your pardon." Harold looked a little pale, as though he expected the aforementioned facer to be delivered at any moment. "We might not make it this time. But we will be married."

"All right! All right!" Ranfield was tired of

his role as righteous guardian. "You've made your point. Now come home. We've a wedding to prepare for."

"A wedding?" Phoebe echoed.

"Yes. Your mama has given her permission."

For a moment the two of them stared at him in shock. Then Harold chuckled. "By Jove," he began. "It actually . . ."

Phoebe gave him a strange look and threw herself into his arms. "Oh Harold, it's so wonderful."

"Yes, yes."

"It actually what?" Ranfield asked.

Harold stuttered. "Ah, a . . . actually going to happen, of course."

Ranfield was not satisfied with this answer. There was something evasive about Harold's eyes.

But Phoebe turned and hurried him up the stairs. "Oh, do let us be going. I can't wait to get home. My wedding! I'm going to plan my wedding. There's so much to do."

Chapter

Seventeen

Aurelia came down to breakfast at the first sign of light. Pratt was already busying himself in the dining room. "No sign of them yet," he said cheerfully. "But they'll be here."

Aurelia looked around. She must be the only one up.

"Mrs. Esterhill is still resting. Your uncle, too. They were up late — talking."

"Thank you, Pratt."

She forced herself to take a cup of tea and a roll. It was difficult getting the roll down past the lump in her throat, but she knew she must eat. There was no telling how long it would take Ranfield to find them. For the hundredth time she asked herself if they had done the right thing. Certainly Phoebe and Harold would be pleased. Their marriage was now assured. And Phoebe's mama would probably keep her word.

But what about Ranfield? She much disliked the way he'd been looking at her. How much did he suspect? And why hadn't she thought of that possibility before she got herself tangled in this briar patch?

Oh, if she only got out of this one, she would never again think of making A Plan!

It was midmorning when the curricle turned into the drive. Aurelia, who had been watching for hours, hurried toward the door. But she was not the first to reach it.

Cousin Prudence was already halfway down the outside stairs, the door ajar behind her.

"I see them!" Pratt exclaimed. "The three of them!" Then, as though remembering his place, he gave Aurelia a subdued look. "That is . . ."

"It's all right, Pratt. Thank God, the Earl has found them."

"Yes, miss. Thank God."

By the time the curricle reached the steps, Cousin Prudence was at the bottom, weeping great tears of joy.

Before the curricle was fairly stopped, Phoebe tumbled out and into her mama's welcoming arms. "Oh, my lamb," moaned Cousin Prudence. "Praise God you're safe."

Phoebe looked uncomfortably close to tears. "Oh, Mama, don't carry on so.

Harold would not let anything harm me. I was always safe."

"Harold . . ." Cousin Prudence stopped suddenly, and seemed to realize that the Earl's eyes were upon her. "Harold will make a good husband, I'm sure." She cast him a look half anger, half tenderness. "But come, Phoebe. We've so much to do."

"Where's Papa?" Harold asked, his expression anxious. Aurelia sighed. The two of them were such babies. She hoped they hadn't already given things away.

"I believe he's out in the shed." She allowed herself a little smile. "He was confident the Earl would find you."

Harold nodded. "I'll just go out there then."

Aurelia turned to follow him, but the Earl said, "Miss Amesley, a moment please."

She wanted to run, but since her legs were so weak that they could hardly hold her, running did not seem a likely solution. She waited, trying to compose herself, while the groom led the stallion away.

The Earl came up and stood in front of her. He seemed so towering, so ferocious. "So, have you no questions for me?"

"Questions? No, milord." Since he was plainly addressing her, she had to raise her eyes to his. His face was expressionless. He

227

stared at her in silence. And yet his voice had conveyed his displeasure quite adequately.

She could feel the blood rising in her cheeks, and finally she could stand his scrutiny no longer. "What is it, milord? Why do you stare at me so?"

He shrugged. "Excuse me. I am merely trying to untangle a puzzle."

"A puzzle?"

"Yes. I find it difficult to understand how Phoebe, who is your bosom bow, could have undertaken such a venture without your knowledge."

Careful now, she must not give herself away. She swallowed. "People in love do strange things."

His smile did not reach his eyes. "So I've been told."

"You talk as though you've never . . ." She stopped, appalled at what she'd been about to say. "I must go, milord. Phoebe will need me."

"Of course."

Later that afternoon, after he had slept a little, Ranfield summoned Phoebe to the library. She hesitated inside the door, plainly nervous.

He gestured. "Sit down. I want to talk to you."

She crossed the room and settled primly on the divan, between the piles of pillows. For a moment silence prevailed. Then she said, "I don't understand. What is there to talk about?"

He swallowed some words unfit for female ears. "What indeed." He fixed her with a stern look. "I want to know who planned this elopement."

"I don't see what difference that makes. It all worked out quite well. You got Mama's consent for us. Oh, thank you, Ranfield, for that. We are very happy."

"That does not answer my question. I cannot believe that Harold would suggest such a thing."

She frowned. "No, no. He didn't."

"Then who did?"

There was only a moment's hesitation, but enough for him to notice it.

"Why, why I did, of course." Her bottom lip quivered slightly and then grew firm. "I love him, you see. And I want to be with him."

"And Aure— Miss Amesley. What part did she play in this?"

"Why, why none at all."

The quiver was more pronounced now. She grabbed up a pillow and hugged it to her. And then she paled and dropped it quickly back. But not before he had seen the book that lay beneath it.

He crossed the room. "What is that?"

"W . . . what?"

He shoved the pillow aside. "This."

"Oh. That's just a romance we were reading. I must have left it in here."

She reached for it, but he was quicker. The cover was worn by much use. She had had it for some time. He studied her face. "Is it good? Shall I read it?"

"Oh no. It's . . . it's very dull."

There was the quiver again. He returned to his chair, taking the book with him.

Phoebe shifted. "Please, Ranfield, may I have my book?"

"Not yet. I want to see how Lady Incognita could be dull."

The book fell open in his hands. Passages were marked in ink. He turned to the back of it. There were some notations — a series of *E*s, of *K*s.

He summoned his sternest look. "All right, Phoebe, enough of this circumvention. I want the truth or your wedding is off."

She turned pale and burst into tears. "Oh, I was so wrong about you. I thought you understood love. But you're a beast . . . a hard unyielding beast. No wonder you can't return Aurelia's love."

The words hit him like a blow. "Can't return . . . ?"

"Yes. I thought you loved her. So did she. For a while. But this proves it. You don't care a fig for her. And now . . . and now . . ."

"Phoebe, my dear." He crossed the room and put an arm around her. "You're wrong. I do love Aurelia."

Her eyes widened. "You do?"

"Yes, I do. But how can I marry a woman who's always in the suds?"

"But that was on purpose."

He felt himself sinking ever deeper into a morass of incomprehensibility. "On purpose?"

"Yes, of course. So you could rescue her."

He shook his head. "I'm afraid I can't understand any of this. Please. Start at the beginning."

She did so, concluding some minutes later by saying, "And we used the book as a model." She took it from him. "These marks show what happened. *E* for embrace. *K* for kiss."

He was overwhelmed by the enormity of their undertaking. "And this plan was to result in a proposal of marriage?"

"Yes, of course." Phoebe sighed. "But after the thing in the caves, Aurelia refused to continue. She feared making you angry."

"And last night's misadventure . . ."

"It was my fault really. She did suggest that *maybe* if we were gone, Mama would change her mind. But it was just a suggestion."

"So you expected me to find you."

"Of course."

He considered this for some moments before he asked, "This Plan. Was there more to it?"

"Yes. But I told you. She refused to go on."

"What was to happen next? Not another runaway."

"Oh, no. Aurelia cannot ride."

"Cannot ride." This piece of information left him almost speechless.

Phoebe patted his hand. "Don't worry, Ranfield. She won't try that again."

"I should hope not. But what . . . ?"

"We had not quite figured it out. I had a brilliant idea. But Aurelia would not hear of it."

And no wonder, considering. Still he had to ask, "What was it?"

"A balloon race. I told her she could go down, and you could rescue her. That would be the big rescue, you see, the one that brings on the declaration of love. And the proposal of matrimony." She sighed.

"But she wouldn't hear of it."

"I see. Phoebe," he said, "lean closer. I have A Plan."

"A race?" Aurelia stared from Ranfield to Phoebe. Phoebe had mentioned a race earlier, but her friend was happily eating a roll, her face the epitome of innocence.

"Yes," Ranfield replied. "All summer you have been touting the advantages of the hydrogen balloon. Now I challenge you to put it to the test."

She frowned. This was not like him. Usually he accepted whatever she said about flight. "But how?"

"We'll go up together. And whoever reaches the other side of the meadow first is the winner. The loser will concede that the winner's choice of propellant is the better."

This scheme was patently ridiculous. "But that will prove nothing . . ."

He gazed at her over the rim of his cup. "Are you reluctant to put your beliefs to the test?"

"Of course not."

He was behaving so strangely. Last evening at dinner he had been silent, hardly saying a word. And now this morning he was overflowing with good spirits.

"But I cannot race," she said. "I promised

Uncle Arthur not to go up alone."

He waved an expansive hand. "You won't be alone. I'll be going up, too."

"But you'll be in the other balloon."

"That will be sufficient. I've spoken to your uncle, and he agrees that for this once it is permissible."

He finished a tremendous plate of ham, eggs, biscuits, and marmalade and emptied his cup. Smiling, he got to his feet. "This afternoon then. Immediately after lunch."

She watched him stride away, so strong, so handsome. And so irritating. She would never understand such a man. But then, what did it matter? After Phoebe and Harold were married, they would return to London — the four of them. And she would devote her life to aeronautical pursuits. At least she would have Phoebe's company.

She looked across the table to where Phoebe was leaning close to Harold. The two looked so happy together. Aurelia swallowed a lump that had risen suddenly in her throat. Phoebe could not have had anything to do with this race idea. She was too engrossed in Harold. Still . . . "Phoebe, may I speak with you?"

Harold grinned and kissed Phoebe's cheek. "Papa's waiting for me in the shed. I'll meet you there later."

Phoebe jumped to her feet and came to give Aurelia a hug. "Oh, it's above all wonderful! We are really and truly going to be married."

"Yes, my dear. But about this race. What do you know about this race?"

"Why nothing, nothing at all. That is, no more than you. But it sounds like fun. Harold says hydrogen is the best for distance. And hot air for short hops."

Aurelia nodded. "He's right. That's why this race will prove very little. Are you sure you had nothing to do with this?"

Phoebe looked aggrieved. "Aurelia, I told you . . . But isn't it strange. Almost like Providence had arranged it." She lowered her voice. "Now, if you were to go off course and come down. Well, who's to say . . . ?"

Aurelia frowned. "Phoebe, I told you. No more rescues."

"But you know what happened when the dark stranger rescued Corrinne." She dimpled. "And it was our rescue from the caves that convinced Harold. He told me so himself. He said he was quite frantic with worry and then he realized he loved me."

Aurelia sighed. "Yes, Phoebe. I admit it worked for you. But Ranfield has no partiality for me. It was all the daydream of some silly young women."

"But The Plan . . ."

With effort, Aurelia crushed a rising inclination to scream. "The Plan was a mistake, the worst mistake of my entire life."

Phoebe put a hand to her temple. "How can you say such a horrid thing? Why, it brought Harold and me together."

Aurelia turned away in exasperation. There was little sense in continuing this conversation, not with Phoebe so set in her thoughts.

"I'm going to meet Mama," Phoebe called after her. "She's promised to come the next time someone goes up. But do think about what I've said."

Gazing after her, Aurelia frowned. It would be an easy matter to go off course. Still . . .

Chapter

Eighteen

They arrived at the meadow in two carriages. Aurelia and Ranfield in the curricle and Phoebe, Cousin Prudence, Uncle Arthur, and Harold in the phaeton. Aurelia was surprised to see Uncle Arthur help Phoebe's mama down. She was even more surprised to see them smiling at each other. They must have reached some kind of truce.

The change that had been wrought in Mrs. Esterhill seemed the next thing to miraculous. Aurelia had expected Phoebe's mama to keep her word, but she had never dreamed she would go about it so happily.

Aurelia stole a glance at the Earl. He had been strangely quiet on the ride, and now his expression was unfathomable.

He turned toward her. "Shall we go?" he asked, gesturing after the others.

"Of course." She grasped her shawl more firmly and prepared to descend from the curricle. But before she could do so, he was there, reaching a hand to help her.

She laid her fingers in his, swallowing the lump that came to her throat. How was she to live without seeing him? He had so inextricably entwined himself with ballooning that it would always make her think of him. But surely she could not be expected to give that up, too.

She focused her attention on Uncle Arthur. She had never seen him looking so delighted. He looked almost gleeful, escorting Cousin Prudence from one balloon to the other, expounding all the while on the science of air flight.

"I cannot quite believe it," Aurelia murmured.

Ranfield chuckled. "It appears that Cousin Prudence has undergone a change of heart."

"It certainly does."

He gave her a most peculiar smile. "I have heard that love makes people do strange things."

"No doubt. But to think that Cousin Prudence's love for her daughter should bring about such a radical change in her beliefs. It is the most amazing thing."

The Earl's smile grew more peculiar. "Yes, it is strange. But come, our public awaits us."

Hearing them approach, Cousin Prudence turned and favored them with a smile. "Milord, I fear I have been sadly mistaken."

"How so?" Ranfield inquired.

"It's this matter of air flight. I am coming to believe the Lord may well be in favor of it."

Aurelia stared. Phoebe's mama looked altogether different. It was true that a bonnet gave her face a different dimension than her habitual cap. But there was something else. Her face had softened somehow. It almost glowed.

"Yes," Cousin Prudence continued. "Arthur has convinced me that flight is practical and safe."

"Of course, it is, Prudence, my dear."

Aurelia almost gasped. Arthur? Prudence? When had the two of them come to the use of Christian names?

"But," Cousin Prudence continued. "It was really the Lord who led me. I opened the Good Book and there it was. Right before my eyes."

"There *what* was?" the Earl inquired politely.

"Why, the verse of course. It says 'and you shall mount up with the wings of the eagle.' These aren't exactly wings. But the idea's the same." She pushed her spectacles up her nose. "Not that I'd ever go up of course." She hesitated and sent Uncle Arthur a girlish smile. "Leastways, not yet. But I'm convinced the Good Lord has nothing against it." And she beamed at the man beside her.

Aurelia considered this new development. Could it possibly be that Uncle Arthur and Cousin Prudence had . . . ? What had Pratt said? That they were up late talking. Well, unlikely as it might seem, it did appear that her uncle and Phoebe's mama were on new, and rather interesting, terms with each other.

But she had no more time to consider this intriguing information. Uncle Arthur turned to her. "We're all ready, Aurelia. Now, you've got to be careful. You know how hydrogen is on short flights."

He took her arm and pulled her aside. "I know you want to win this race, but winning ain't everything. I'm only letting you go up alone because . . ." He frowned. "Because this seems so important to the Earl. And it's a short hop." He patted her arm. "Don't put yourself in danger, my dear. We don't need to win. We *know* hydrogen is better."

"Yes, Uncle Arthur. I understand."

Following him to the balloon, Aurelia tried to bring some order out of the chaos of her thoughts. All morning she'd been reminding herself that another accident was out of the question. Another such debacle would set the Earl's back up permanently. And yet . . . The Plan had worked for Phoebe.

Aurelia pressed a hand to her throbbing temple. If only she knew what to do. If only she could be sure.

"Come," said Harold, giving her his arm. "Ranny is most ready." He led her toward the balloon. "Now, don't you worry none," he said. "It don't matter if Ranny wins this race. We know hydrogen is better."

"Why . . ."

Harold patted her hand. "No time for that. The balloons are ready. See, here comes Ranny now."

"But . . ." But Harold was already gone, hurrying to Phoebe's side and tucking her arm through his.

Approaching Aurelia, Ranfield frowned. She looked a little on the green side. "Are you ill?"

She shook her head. "No, no. It's just the excitement. So, milord. Where is the finish line for this race of yours?"

He gestured. "At the other end of the meadow. My men have spread a red blanket. Anchored it with stones. Are you sure . . . ?"

"I'm quite well, thank you."

Her tone was testy and she looked decidedly peaked. But this was not the time to pursue the matter. Perhaps it *was* the excitement of the race. She'd looked fine at breakfast. "Very well, then. Shall we begin?"

"Yes, of course. Harold will help me into the gondola."

He nodded and made his way to his own balloon. Perhaps he was being foolhardy, trying to arrange the romantic scene she longed for. He wasn't even sure she was going to follow The Plan. Phoebe thought so. But Phoebe was so lovestruck she was hardly a good judge of anything.

He swung a leg over the side of the basket. He should have arranged a nice ride . . . Lord, no, not the way she rode. But perhaps a picnic. Still, with the others around it was almost impossible to get her alone. And he could hardly put the question to her in company.

Damnation! He couldn't wait much longer. He was going to ask her. This very day. No matter what.

"Ready?" Harold called.

Ranfield looked to her. She was nodding. He waved his own hand.

"Then go!"

The servants released the ropes and

slowly the balloons rose. Ranfield, feeding straw to the brazier's fire, glanced at Aurelia's balloon. It was rising at about the same speed as his own. He watched her peer over the edge, intent on seeing the red blanket that was their goal.

Could she really love him? Or was Phoebe just imagining the whole thing? But the marks had been there in the book. And Aurelia's accidents had occurred.

She was testing the air currents. He should be doing the same. He squinted against the sun, trying to make out her features. But she was too far away.

He would have to stay in the same current in order to be there for the final rescue. But what if Phoebe was mistaken? What if Aurelia didn't fake an accident? There was her pride to be considered. Ballooning was her life, and all summer she had been a passionate advocate of hydrogen gas.

Damnation! His balloon was going the wrong way. It was headed not toward the other end of the meadow but at right angles to it, back toward the house. He added more straw to the brazier. The balloon rose, but it still kept its direction.

In the other balloon, Aurelia muttered softly and pulled on the valve rope. What on earth was he doing? It was dangerous to head back toward those trees. She waved her arms and made motions for him to go up, but he was intent on feeding the brazier and didn't see her.

With a sigh, she dumped some ballast till she rose to his height. Wherever he was going, she would follow.

They went for some distance and then his balloon began to descend, not slowly and gracefully, but in erratic dips and dives that made her catch her breath. She pulled the valve rope and followed him down, her eyes on the terrain below.

The house was still far away, but almost beneath them was the stream where the horse had thrown her. For a moment she let herself think about that precious day. But his balloon tangled in the nearby trees. His gondola hit the earth and bounced. She almost screamed as the hot coals flew from the brazier and hissed into the stream. And then a figure tumbled from the rolling basket, to lie still at the water's edge.

"Ranfield! Oh, no!"

Heedless of her own safety or that of the balloon, Aurelia brought it swiftly down into a thicket. She was out of the gondola almost before it hit the ground and racing through the brambles to the streambed.

He lay half in the water, his upturned face

pale. With a shudder she dragged him to dry ground. Then she knelt beside him, but he did not open his eyes. "Oh, dear. It's all my fault. I should never have agreed to this flight."

She lifted his head to her lap and pressed a kiss to his brow. "Oh, what shall I do without you?" she murmured. "How shall I ever live?"

His eyes fluttered and opened. "Aurelia?"

The sound of her name brought tears to her eyes. "Yes, Ranfield, I am here."

"What happened?"

"Your balloon came down. You were tipped out."

He stared up at her. "And you came down after me?"

"Well, yes. I . . . I saw that you were injured."

He put his hand to his head. "A little bump, nothing more." He pushed himself to a sitting position facing her. "So you rescued me."

"Oh, milord, it was . . ."

He began to laugh. In consternation she watched as his laughter grew and grew. "Ranfield? Milord?"

"You . . . rescued . . . me. Oh, that . . . is . . . rich."

His laughter reached out and caught her,

pulling her into his mirth. And soon she was laughing, too. Just as they had that day in the stream.

She did not know quite when it happened, but somehow, some way, his arms were around her. And hers around him. And still they laughed.

Finally, she raised her head from where it lay against his soggy waistcoat. "I . . . Why do we laugh like this?"

His eyes were so bright, pieces of heaven shining in his beloved face.

"I cannot speak for you," he said, his expression sobering. "But I know perfectly well why I feel so fine."

Her heart began those wild palpitations again. "You do?"

"Oh, yes." He pulled her closer against him. "It's because I love you, Aurelia Amesley."

For a moment she thought the breath had left her lungs forever. And then she could speak again, but she could not believe. "What did you say?"

He looked down at her, his expression tender. "I said I love you."

"You . . . love . . . me," she repeated woodenly. She had never swooned in her life, but she felt dangerously close to it.

His face darkened. "Phoebe was right,

wasn't she? If that chit misled me . . ."

"Phoebe?" Her voice was sharper than she intended. "What has Phoebe to do with this?"

His eyes clouded. "She said . . . She assured me . . ." He withdrew his arm and sat stiffly apart. "I seem to have made a mistake, Miss Amesley. My cousin misread your feelings for me. She mistook gratitude for affection and . . ."

He looked so miserable, she could not bear it. "Phoebe," she began, but he was so firmly launched into abject apology that he could not hear her. And so, with complete disregard for propriety and The Plan, she threw herself into his arms. Never having done such a thing before, she threw herself rather more emphatically than necessary with the result that he ended flat on his back and she on top of him. But she did not let that deter her. Promptly she pressed her lips to his.

It was a most satisfying kiss, far better than the one he had given her in the balloon. For one thing, now she knew what to expect. And for another, he had said he loved her.

When she raised her mouth, he was staring at her in the most bewildered fashion. "Ranfield," she said. "I love you, too."

His smile began then and grew to such proportions that she almost burst into laughter again. But there were too many questions still unanswered.

She pushed herself to a sitting position. Once she was off him, he got immediately to his feet.

"What . . . ?"

And then he dropped to one knee in front of her. A giggle threatened to choke her. He pretended a thunderous glare. "If you insist on laughing at me, how shall I do this thing properly?" He took her hand. "Miss Amesley. Aurelia. My love. Will you marry me?"

The lump in her throat was so big she had to struggle to get the words over it. "Yes, yes I will."

"Did I do it properly? Shall I add anything?"

"Oh, no, my love. It was perfect. The most perfect proposal a woman ever received."

He dropped to the grass beside her and wiped his brow. "I'm glad that's over. My darling, I'm sorry it didn't work out as you wished."

"As I wished?"

"Yes, Phoebe told . . ."

"Phoebe told . . ."

"Come, love." He put his arm around

her. "It was not her fault. You know she cannot stand up under my glare."

"She told you about The Plan." Aurelia did not know whether to laugh or cry. "Oh, it is so mortifying."

"Nonsense." He kissed her hand. "Actually, it was very enterprising. Though completely unnecessary."

"Unnecessary?"

"Yes, sweet. You see I loved you the first moment I saw you."

She remembered that moment — the meeting of their eyes in Hyde Park. "Ranfield . . ."

"I did not know it then, of course. Until you crashed into my stables. And my dearest, now that you are to be my wife, will you not call me Philip?"

"Yes, Philip. But why . . . ?" She found to her surprise that she could now ask him anything. "Why did you take so long?"

"Because of The Plan, my dear." He kissed the tip of her nose. "The Plan almost persuaded me that you were too scatter-brained to be my wife. First you crash into my stables. I know, that was really an accident." He laughed. "But my love, the way you ride a horse . . . I wonder that that accident wasn't fatal."

"I know. You will have to teach me properly. But really, Philip, I did not intend to knock you breathless that day in the meadow."

He kissed her chin. "And Phoebe's escapade in the caves was *her* idea." He frowned. "Though I understand you had something to do with the elopement."

"A little. I just thought that Phoebe's mama might come round when she thought she'd lost her altogether."

He pulled her closer. "And you were right. I understand, my love. And I promise I shall continue to supply you with romances of terror."

"You shall?"

"Oh, yes. But I require one pledge in return."

She snuggled comfortably against him. "What pledge is that?"

"I insist that you no longer try to live these romances. I would like to enjoy our life together without benefit of added hazards."

And then it hit her. Her ballooning. "You won't . . . ? I can't . . . ."

"Of course not, my love." His smile made her blood sing. "We will continue ballooning. I shall even convert my balloon to hydrogen gas . . . if that pleases you. But one more thing."

"Yes?"

"We must always go up together. I cannot bear it otherwise."

Feeling greatly daring, she kissed the point of his chin. "Of course, Philip. We'll do everything together. And I do promise I'll give up living romances. But you must admit that The Plan was not such a bad thing."

"How so?"

"Well, it brought Harold and Phoebe together. And, however obliquely, us. So, in the long run it worked admirably."

He chuckled. "More admirably even than you suppose. This morning your uncle came to me about Prudence. It appears that he's gotten used to her Scriptures and now that she's been converted to air flight, he means to ask her the question."

"Three. Three marriages," Aurelia said triumphantly. "And all from one Plan."

From the distance came the sound of breaking branches. "Hal-loo. Ree-ly? Ranny? Are you there?"

"Yes, Harold," the Earl shouted. "We're both here. And doing very well." Then he took her in his arms and kissed her yet again.

The employees of Thorndike Press hope you have enjoyed this Large Print book. All our Large Print titles are designed for easy reading, and all our books are made to last. Other Thorndike Press Large Print books are available at your library, through selected bookstores, or directly from the publishers.

For more information about titles, please call:

(800) 223-1244
(800) 223-6121

To share your comments, please write:

Publisher
Thorndike Press
295 Kennedy Memorial Drive
Waterville, Maine 04901